**Trentor's head was up,
and he was sniffing the wind.**

"There is something quite close by that I do not like," he said.

Loro felt his throat ache and he swallowed.

"What is it?" Ria asked.

"I don't know," Trentor said, "but whatever it is, it's small and fast."

"Maybe it's not a meat eater," Ria said hopefully. "Maybe it lives in the marshes because there are so many plants."

"Perhaps," Trentor said. "But—"

Suddenly, twin screeches sliced through the humid air. Loro spun around to see two forms roughly half Trentor's size scurrying through the brush. They leaped out of the shadows, straight at them.

"Run!" Loro shouted.

VISIT THE EXCITING WORLD OF

IN THESE BOOKS:

DINOTOPIA
RESCUE PARTY

by Mark A. Garland

Random House 🏠 New York

To Harry and Mae Hudson—M.G.
The publisher's special thanks to James, Jeanette, and Dan Gurney

www.randomhouse.com/kids
www.dinotopia.com

Library of Congress Catalog Card Number: 97-76478
ISBN: 0-679-89107-2
RL: 5.3

Printed in the United States of America 10 9 8 7 6 5 4

DINOTOPIA IS A REGISTERED TRADEMARK OF JAMES GURNEY

Cover illustration by Michael Welply

RESCUE PARTY

Windy Point

Crystal Caverns •

The Hatchery •

Baz ••

Pooktook •

Volcaneum •

Hadro Swamp

Waterfall City •

Sculpted Cliffs •

The Time Towers

Cornucopia •   *Deep Lake*
Treetown •   • Bent Root

Temple Ruins •

RAINY
BASIN

GREAT CANAL

SKY GALLEY CAVES •

Tentpole of the Sky •

Sky City •

Thermala •

Polongo River

NORTHERN PLAINS

BACKBONE MOUNTAINS

Rocky Pass

Prosperine •

Sapphire Bay
• Poseidos
(sunken)

Amu River

Pteros •

Canyon City •

Ancient Gorge

Red Rapid
Canyon

The Sentinels

*Warmwater
Bay*

Culebra •

OUTER ISLAND

CRACKSHELL POINT

FORBIDDEN MOUNTAINS

The Portal

GREAT DESERT

• Sauropolis

Dolphin Bay

BLACKWOOD
FLATS

• Chandara

Dragonfly Coast

Cape Turtletail

CHAPTER 1

Ankla took a slow, deep breath. The Brachiosaur's huge midsection expanded even more, nearly knocking Loro off the rolling scaffold on which he stood. Loro recovered his balance, then used one of the ropes draped over Ankla's back to pull the scaffold snug again.

Ankla looked back at Loro and exhaled. Loro's short brown hair fluttered in the breeze.

"Still there?" she asked.

Loro laughed. Ankla's voice consisted more of great, hollow rumbles than actual words. That was how most dinosaurs talked. Like all humans in Dinotopia, Loro had long ago learned to understand them.

"I'm fine," he said, already scrubbing again. He was almost finished washing his side of the massive Brachiosaur, one of the oldest in the village. "I've got perfect balance."

"How do you do that without a tail?" asked someone on the ground.

Loro glanced down to see his friend Trentor looking up at him. Trentor was a young Styracosaurus. He and Loro—and Ria, too—had been friends forever. Ria was Loro's stepsister, though, which was different.

Just then, Ria came walking around Ankla. She had been washing the Brachiosaur's other side.

"That's easy," she said, answering Trentor. "We don't have to walk on our hands!" She held her arms out and walked a straight line, tightrope-style.

Trentor just shook his head. Ria laughed as she wiped the sweat from her forehead.

Loro grinned. He was glad he'd been working on the dinosaur's shady side. The spring afternoon was warm and sunny, and the breeze was filled with the smell of wild blossoms—which did a fair job of covering the aroma of the barn's nearby dung heap. It was the first time in weeks they'd been able to move their washing and scrubbing out of the huge barn where Ankla usually slept.

Trentor stood silently for a moment, apparently trying to think up a clever response. Then he tipped his head and pointed his three horns toward a row of saddles on a nearby fence.

"All well and good," he said, grinning with just the corners of his mouth. That was all his bony face would allow. "But let's try putting one of those saddles on your back and letting *you* carry *me!*"

Loro chuckled. It was true; Trentor carried Loro and Ria everywhere. Ria looked up at Loro and bowed, which meant it was up to him. Loro could think pretty fast when he had to.

"Sure," said Loro, "but *you* try climbing up here and washing Ankla's back or cinching up the straps on those saddles."

"All well and good," Trentor said, "but *you* try—"

Ankla groaned. "You three will never stop," she said. She waved her sinuous neck back and forth as if her head hurt. Then she nudged the wash bucket with her nose. "That, or you'll never finish."

"Almost done," Loro said, going back to his scrubbing. It was just as well. Trentor was good at their game of "better than"; he had a very logical mind. Most dinosaurs did. After all, they had several million years' head start on human beings.

"I'll finish her hind legs," Ria said, dipping her brush in the bucket and getting started.

"You two always do such a wonderful job," Ankla said.

"Start at the top and work your way down," Loro recited. That was the only proper way to wash a dinosaur, especially one with a neck that reached forty feet in the air—higher, if Ankla stood on her haunches.

The giant Brachiosaurs were among Bonabba's most important residents. When fitted head to toe with handmade plates of armor, they were *the* essential part of any caravan that hoped to travel through the Rainy Basin. The thick jungles of the Basin were home to Dinotopia's least sociable inhabitants, meat eaters like Giganotosaurus and Tyrannosaurus rex.

Loro had never actually seen any of the big meat

eaters. Bonabba was separated from the Basin by a deep ravine, and Loro was not allowed to cross the drawbridge that spanned it. But he'd heard them calling to one another: long, deep howls or short, rising roars that drifted for miles on the still night air.

Loro sighed and looked up at the sky. He'd never been much of anywhere, really, and that was the trouble. When he had time, he liked to sit by the bridge and look out over the ravine. Or he'd lie back and watch the clouds pass overhead, sky travelers. By night he'd watch the stars, listen to the sounds of the jungle, and dream of things to come. Which reminded him...

"Ankla?" Loro asked. "Would you tell us again about your journey to the Tomb of Mujo Doon?"

Ria groaned. "Haven't we heard that one at least a dozen times already?" she teased.

"I have told the story often," Ankla said. "And it *is* rather long."

"But it's so good!" Loro said.

"Yes, often, long, and good," Trentor said, agreeing with everyone.

"Every story Ankla tells is good," said Ria.

That was true. Ankla had been to every corner of Dinotopia. She'd seen so much. It was almost too exciting for Loro to imagine.

"Never mind," Loro said, returning to his scrubbing. Even though Dinotopia was his home, he'd seen very little of it, and he could only imagine the land he'd come from.

Loro had lived in Dinotopia for most of his thirteen years, but he hadn't been born there. When he was still just a baby, the dolphins had saved him from a shipwreck, as they had saved so many others over the centuries. Ria's mother had adopted Loro and raised him and Ria as brother and sister.

Loro had been told this many times, and he knew in his heart that it was true. Distant places had always called to him. He could hear the voice of the unknown in his dreams, and he could feel it in his bones.

Trentor spoke up from below. "As soon as you're done here," he said, "I was hoping you two could help me with my chores. I want to be finished before dinner so I can go to the concert tonight."

"Of course," Ria said.

Loro nodded. He'd forgotten about the concert. It was to feature several of Bonabba's most talented Hadrosaurs. Hadrosaurs could produce a beautiful range of musical tones through their hollow skull crest. The new tenor was supposed to be quite good.

Even so, Loro was pretty sure he'd been to too many concerts. He sighed and started to climb down.

"What's wrong?" asked Trentor.

Loro shrugged. "Do you realize how many times we've gone to these concerts?"

Trentor cocked his head to one side. "No," he said. "Why?"

"Uh-oh," Ria said. She put her brush in the

bucket and dried her hands on her pants. "I think I know what's coming."

"It's nothing, really," Loro said, putting his brush away as well. "It's just that, no matter how nice something is, sometimes you'd rather be doing something else."

"Uh-oh," Trentor said, finally catching on.

Ankla snorted—this was her version of a laugh. "Thank you for doing such a nice job," she said. "Now, if you'll excuse me, I'm in the mood for a nap."

She slowly moved off toward the barn.

"You're welcome," Ria told her.

"Good-bye," Trentor called after her.

"I still would like to have heard another story," Loro muttered.

"You're not bored, are you, little brother?" Ria asked.

Loro just shrugged.

Ria wrinkled her nose at him. "Too bad!" she said. "Bonabba is boring only if you make it that way. I find plenty to keep me busy."

"You mean busybody," Loro teased.

Ria planted her hands on her hips and showed him her deepest scowl. She loved their village and everyone and everything in it. In fact, Loro sometimes thought that Ria considered herself personally responsible for all of Bonabba—especially him.

"I'm just interested in people, that's all," she said.

"Well, so am I," Loro replied. "But Bonabba isn't

6

the whole world. All of Dinotopia is out there, just waiting! But here I sit, day after day, night after night—"

"And that's just what you'll keep doing, if you know what's good for you," Ria said. "At least for a little while yet."

"When you are older," Trentor said to him, slowly and steadily as usual, "you will do many exciting things. All of us will. One day, I will become a cross-Basin trail guide like my father, and I will have many stories to tell, but only when it is time, and only when he has taught me all that I need to know. Then, you will come and share that time with me. You have the spirit of a great adventurer. I don't think it will be wasted."

Loro nodded slowly. "You're right, I guess. But aren't you eager to get out there right now?"

"I can wait for the proper day."

"Oh," said Loro. He didn't quite understand how. Trentor could recite in complete detail every one of the stories his father, Fraalor, had ever told him. And he had assembled one of the best map collections in all of Dinotopia. Yet he was still content to wait.

Every time Loro heard another wondrous tale of some far-off place, or reread the accounts of Arthur Denison's famous expeditions, or looked at any of Trentor's maps, he felt a familiar stirring inside that would not let him be.

"Well," Ria said, "If you were somewhere else,

you'd be dreaming about coming to Bonabba. Because we are somewhere already." She lifted her chin and sniffed at him.

Loro frowned. "I just want to explore new places."

"Like where?" Ria asked.

"How about the Rainy Basin?" said Loro.

"I knew you'd say that!" Ria said. "Do you know how dangerous that would be?"

"I understand how you feel," Trentor said to Loro. "But it is a very human thing, I think."

"A very *boy* human thing," Ria scoffed.

"Perhaps," Trentor said. "But, Loro, such a journey would be very dangerous indeed. There are many things that could go wrong. You could be eaten. You might get lost. You might starve, or die of thirst, or take ill with no one to tend to you. And if you crossed the Basin and reached the mountains, well, then the snow and the cold would find you."

"I suppose," Loro said, kicking the ground with his toe.

Ria put her hand on Loro's shoulder. "You know we're right," she said.

Loro only sighed. Ria planned to grow up to be the region's Habitat Partner or to have a seat at the annual Habitat Conference. Or maybe she'd design a new city from scratch, like the Greek and Roman settlers in times past, or invent a new game that every inhabitant of the island could play.

Loro knew that *somebody* had to do those things.

Dinotopia needed its builders, its planners, its spirited busybodies. He just didn't want to be one of them. After all, Dinotopia needed explorers, too.

"Be thankful for today," Ria recited. It meant about the same to her as "Breathe deep, seek peace," a favorite greeting throughout the land.

"I am thankful," Loro said. "It's not that. I just feel like it's time to face danger, beat the odds, learn new things. It's time to find answers to questions we haven't even thought of yet!"

"If you have no question, you need no answer," Trentor counseled evenly, his armored head bobbing up and down in a gentle nod. "Meanwhile, one must wait for the proper time and strive to be prepared."

"But we've all been taught how to survive in the jungle," Loro said. "We've played 'caravan' since we were babies, and we know every cross-Basin trail story by heart. Don't you ever wonder how you'd do if you actually went out there?"

"Not really," Ria said. "There's too much going on around here, like the concert."

Loro's shoulders slumped. "I know," he said. "After the concert, do you think maybe we could go out to the bridge and try to spot something in the jungle? It'll be a full moon tonight. While we're there, maybe we could plan just a *little* trip..."

"I would like to do all of that," Trentor said. "But if I get to sleep too late, the next day I am so tired. And I have a lot of chores to do."

"I don't know," Ria said. "I think you already have enough plans in your head without our help."

Suddenly, Loro's frustration overwhelmed him. "Maybe," he said. "Or maybe I'm just growing up, and you're still thinking like a kid!"

He knew it was the wrong thing to say the moment he'd said it. Ria gave him her "you're forgetting who's the boss" look, a look that smoldered like embers.

"I'm telling Mom," she said.

"Fine," said Loro, trying to sound unconcerned. "I don't care."

"Fine!" Ria said with a sniff. She turned and stomped off toward the village pod houses.

Trentor looked at Ria, then at Loro, then at Ria again. He shook his head.

"There are some things about humans I will never understand," he said.

"Me neither," said Loro. "Me neither."

CHAPTER 2

"He actually scares me sometimes," Ria said. She reached into the laundry basket and pulled out a blouse. "All he thinks about is rushing off on some great adventure."

"Loro has an explorer's spirit," said Trentor.

"True enough," Ria's mother, Katherine, said. She pinned a pair of Ria's pants up on the clothesline, then bent and pulled the last pair out of the basket. One end of the clothesline was attached to a T-shaped wooden pole. The other end ran directly into the trunk of the tree in which Katherine, Ria, and Loro's pod house sat.

"One day," Katherine said, "I'm sure he will find something wonderful."

"But this is today," Ria said. "Lately, he doesn't seem the least bit interested in anything that goes on here. If Trentor and I didn't keep talking him out of it, he'd have us prowling around in the Rainy Basin or flying off on the next Skybax."

"Do you think that's the only reason he doesn't

go?" Katherine asked, picking up the empty basket.

"I guess," Ria said.

"Well," Katherine said, "even though he acts brave and talks adventure, I don't think he's about to go strolling in the Rainy Basin alone. For now I'd say he's mostly just talk."

"Loro doesn't want to explore just the Basin," Ria said. "He wants to explore the entire world!"

Katherine shrugged. "Perhaps one day he will."

"Not one day," Ria replied. "Right now."

"You sound so worried," Katherine said, tipping her head and considering her daughter. "Why is that?"

Ria shrugged. "He's just being ridiculous lately," she said. "Especially since the weather started to warm up. Every night he wants to sit down by the bridge and listen to the jungle."

"Yes," Trentor said, "but I like to listen, too. And he does tell many fine stories while we sit there. Tales he's heard passing travelers tell, and some he just makes up for fun. Then it is our turn, and I tell the stories I know. I tell my father's stories over and over."

Trentor sounded much too cheery. Not that Ria didn't like that about him—sometimes, Trentor could find the sunny side of the darkest cloud. But you could also count on Trentor to point out everything that was worth worrying about. *That* was the Trentor Ria needed right now.

"Everyone enjoys those stories," Katherine said. "I think maybe Loro just loves them a bit more."

"Just a bit," Ria said, rolling her eyes.

Katherine laughed. "Very well," she said. "But we have to remember that Loro is going to be whoever he was meant to be, and he must learn who that is for himself, just as we all must. Though for him it may be especially hard. Unlike you or Trentor, Loro has no one to tell him of his ancestry, his people, or his home. We never knew his parents, but if they were on a ship at sea, then we can guess they were adventurers of a sort. Adventure must run in his blood."

Trentor nodded. Ria finally did the same.

"Meanwhile," Katherine went on, "I'd like you two to promise me you'll keep an eye on him. Make sure he doesn't get himself into too much trouble."

"I promise," Ria said. After all, if someone had to keep an eye on Loro, she ought to be the one!

Ria watched her mother go back into the house. Then she turned to Trentor and said, "Okay, let's go find him."

Trentor turned his eyes skyward as they set out across the village. Ria followed his gaze. The late-afternoon sky was filling with dark, angry-looking clouds, and a cool breeze had begun to blow. If it rained too heavily there wouldn't be any concert at all—a thought which didn't exactly please Ria. No concert meant that she'd end up sitting around the house with Loro, listening to him read aloud from Arthur Denison's notes again.

"I think a storm is brewing," Trentor said.

"Don't even say it," Ria scolded. "You'll bring one on for sure."

"I don't see how."

"Oh, you know what I mean," Ria said. "Now come on, let's get going."

The two of them made their way across the village, giving Ria a chance to visit with everyone.

"You guys are gonna hurt somebody!" she scolded, as two young boys ran past. Then Sara, a girl a year younger than Ria, came walking toward them.

"How is your rock garden coming along?" Ria asked her.

"Okay," Sara said. "But I can't get the red ferns to grow. They keep turning brown."

"I'll come over tomorrow," Ria said. "We'll either kill them or save them."

"Great!" Sara said, grinning. "I was hoping you'd say that. You always seem to know what to do."

Ria just smiled.

Trentor and Ria soon passed a group of saurians and humans discussing preparations for a birthday feast.

"Oh, I'd love to help plan the party," Ria told Trentor, as they slowed and listened.

"Then why don't you?" Trentor asked.

"Because I'd get caught up in it," said Ria. "I could easily spend the whole day doing just that."

Trentor considered the group. "I know the Diplodocus," he said. "We could visit them later."

"So I can catch up on all the details!" Ria said, quite pleased. Trentor nodded, and the two of them picked up their pace once more.

They finally reached the Skybax perch at the southern edge of town. No Skybax were in sight. They came more frequently in the summer months, though even then only occasionally. But that didn't stop Loro from hanging around the large landing perch, just in case a winged shadow should happen to cross over.

Ria and Trentor found him there. He was sitting on the edge of the high perch, gazing toward the distant jungle. He glanced down at his visitors.

"Did you miss me?" Loro asked.

"A little," Ria said. He'd be up there forever unless she could get him to come down and join the world again. Just part of her job, she told herself.

"Are you having fun?" she asked.

"You can see a long way from up here," he said. "That's what I like about it."

"You can also fall a long way if you aren't careful," Ria said.

"I know," Loro said, "but I'm always careful."

Ria folded her arms across her chest and looked at Trentor. "Did he say 'always'?" she asked.

"And careful," Trentor said.

Ria looked up at Loro again. "Don't you ever get bored?" Ria asked.

"Sometimes," Loro called out. "But it's well worth

15

it if a Skybax lands, and I'm the first to greet the rider."

"And if none show, which they rarely do, you will have wasted the whole day," Ria said.

Loro frowned down at her. "I wouldn't expect you to understand," he said. Then he pulled back from the edge of the perch, out of sight.

"I think he is staying up there," Trentor said.

Ria sighed. "Now what do we do?"

She examined the brooding gray skies once more. The breeze had died. In fact, the air was utterly still. Something about it raised the hair on the back of her neck. In the distance, far out over the ocean, she could see dim flashes of lightning, and at that very moment the first faint rumbles of thunder found her ears. The storm was taking a long time to build, which meant that it would probably be a bad one. Suddenly the wind started to blow, and the blackest of the clouds flickered with fire.

"On the other hand," Ria said, setting her jaw. "Something tells me he'll be down in no time. We're all about to get soaked!"

CHAPTER 3

Loro was imagining for the thousandth time what it would be like to fly over the Basin jungles when a loud crack of thunder broke behind him. He turned and looked at the sky. Suddenly a bright flash of lightning burst through the darkness. The storm would arrive in minutes, and a high perch was nowhere for him to be when it did.

He scrambled down off the tower and brushed past Ria and Trentor. He found his friends matching his pace on either side of him.

"I told Mom, you know," Ria said.

"But you didn't say she was angry," Loro said. A sudden gust of wind at his back spurred him into a jog. His companions started to jog as well. The next gust was even stronger.

Others around the village, human and saurian alike, were gathering belongings left out in their yards and closing the shutters on their windows before heading for the sauropod barns for shelter.

The wind was blowing dust into Loro's eyes, making them water, and the air had become much cooler.

"The wind is coming around, switching directions," Trentor said. "I don't remember it ever being this strong."

"Me neither," Ria agreed. She tipped her head into the force of the wind and shielded her face with one hand.

"Maybe so, but..." Loro stopped and waved his arms at the thick clouds racing overhead. "I think it's kind of exciting! Don't you?"

He watched the look on Ria's face turn from a squint to scorn and knew his remark had had the desired effect. She wanted to hurry, and he wanted her to stop trying to run his life.

"*I* do not find this exciting," Trentor cautioned. "Think what could happen! We could be hit by lightning, or flying objects, or hail, or—"

"I know, I know," Loro said.

"Then let's get going!" Ria shouted, grabbing Loro's shirt and tugging him forward.

"I can walk all by myself, thank you," Loro said.

Ria glared at him. She looked as though she were about to explode. Loro felt a guilty twinge of satisfaction.

"Then you do just that!" Ria said. She turned and set out again, toward home.

"Go ahead," Loro told Trentor, waving the saurian on. "I'm coming."

Trentor turned and did as Loro had said, though

judging by the droop of his bony head he wasn't happy about it.

Loro waited just long enough to make his point. He had no intention of standing around like a human lightning rod any longer than he had to. Already, everyone in the entire village had taken cover. He could see the giant doors closing on the nearest of the sauropod barns. A chill went through him. *Time to get going!*

But he found it hard to make headway. The wind was so strong that he could hardly stand up, let alone run forward. He lowered his body as close to the ground as he could manage and forced his way through the wind. *Head for the nearest shelter,* he thought.

The branches of nearby trees twisted and snapped, and a spray of leaves pelted Loro. The tangy, metallic smell of rain filled his nose as he turned toward the barn where Ankla lived. He was scared now, more so than he could ever remember. He'd never seen a storm anything like this one, and it was only getting started.

Then Loro heard a deafening crack. He flinched as the heat and flash of a lightning bolt surrounded him, followed instantly by a tremendous explosion.

The wind rushed at him again, as if pushed by a giant's hand, and knocked him on his back. A spray of dust stung his face and burned his eyes as he gasped for air. Then he heard another cracking sound, different than the first, coming from somewhere just above…

He tried to open his eyes, blinked, and caught a glimpse of something large and dark sailing through the air. It was a giant tree limb!

A sharp pain filled Loro's chest as it landed on him. It had to be half a tree, Loro thought. He couldn't move.

Loro tried to call for help, but he couldn't breathe deeply enough to speak. *Calm down*, he told himself. *Think.*

He discovered that he could wiggle his fingers and toes. That was a good sign, but other than that he was trapped. Loro's thoughts began to run wild. He'd never panicked before, but he was sure this was what panic was like. He was losing control of his mind!

Water started to fall on him in waves. It soaked the ground, instantly creating standing water. His head was turned slightly to one side, and he couldn't quite straighten it. If the water got high enough to cover his mouth…

"Loro!"

He opened his eyes. Rain stabbed into them, but he saw a shape—no, two shapes!—standing over him.

"Loro, hold on and we'll help you!"

He recognized the voice. It was Ria!

Loro tried harder to focus. The larger shape standing just behind Ria was Trentor.

"Push, Trentor!" Ria howled. Trentor wedged his

bony nose against the massive limb. The powerful Styracosaurus grunted and groaned as he pushed with all his strength. Ria had her shoulder against the limb close beside Trentor.

"You have to help!" Ria cried out. Loro nodded. The other two dipped down and made contact with the limb, and Loro joined in with every ounce of strength he could gather.

"Heave!" Ria screamed. Loro felt the limb moving, then he saw smaller branches and leaves whipping around just above him. He tried to move...

And did!

Not very far, and everything hurt. About the best he could do was roll and flop in the mud like a fresh-caught fish. But he got out from under the tree far enough so that Ria and Trentor could let it go.

"I've got you," Ria said, getting her arm under him and helping him up. "Get hold of Trentor!"

Loro wrapped his arm around the top of Trentor's muzzle and found himself being dragged toward the same barn he'd been heading for in the first place. A moment later they were through the giant door.

"You're just lucky we decided to go back for you," Ria said, as Loro felt the last of his strength drain out of him. He slipped down, off Trentor's side, unable to stop himself. Ria put her arms under him and slowed his fall, then helped him lie down on a bed of straw.

"You were in quite a mess," Trentor said. "But this is just the kind of thing that can happen when you take chances with a storm this bad. I tried to tell you."

"Well, I tried to tell him, too," Ria said.

It didn't sound as if she were gloating, Loro thought. Just saying so, loud and clear. After all, he deserved it.

Outside, the winds howled and buffeted the building with growing force. Loro listened to the heavy rattle of the barn's main door and the moaning of the walls as they were stretched to their limit. It sounded bad, and for the first time he began to wonder about the survival of the village itself and everyone in it.

Suddenly he heard a roar somewhere behind him, followed by a series of sickening cracking sounds, and he knew the building's roof was coming off.

CHAPTER 4

The last thing Loro saw was Ankla and Ronan, another Brachiosaur, reaching up with their long necks and pushing large bales of straw into an opening in the roof. After that, Loro closed his eyes for a moment...

When he opened his eyes again, all was quiet. Loro glanced around, but the barn was empty. He tried to sit up and instantly wished he hadn't. His head hurt as much as his chest, which felt as if a Skybax had landed on it.

No matter, Loro told himself. He got slowly to his feet. He discovered he could walk and breathe all right, but it wasn't easy. At least he was all in one piece. But where had everyone gone?

"Looks like you're going to live."

Loro looked up and saw Ria standing in the doorway. She grinned at him.

"I...I guess so," Loro said, discovering that it even hurt to talk.

"I've been keeping an eye on you," Ria said. She

gestured toward the door. "Come have a look."

Loro made his way to the doorway and looked outside. He couldn't believe his eyes. The village was a shambles.

Every human and saurian in Bonabba was at work, trying to put the community back together again. Many pod houses had had their roofs torn off. Some had collapsed altogether. Most of the saurian barns were damaged as well. Trees and other debris lay everywhere, all of it rain-soaked and muddy.

Loro turned toward the southern end of the village and saw that there was nothing left of the Skybax perch but a few poles. Among the trees just beyond the perch he spotted one of the heavy wooden carts used to haul straw and dung. It was turned upside down and stuck high in a tree!

Looking north across the village's small pond, he spotted a dinosaur resting on its haunches. Two people were working on one of its legs, applying a very large bandage. Then one of the older men in the village walked by. The man's granddaughter was leading him, and he was dragging one leg, using a stick as a cane. Loro's thoughts were suddenly filled with worries about his friends, his home, and his mother.

"He is up and about!" said another familiar voice. Trentor came padding up beside Ria and tipped his horned head to one side, apparently inspecting Loro for damage. "And all in one piece."

He sounded glad. They both did. Loro remembered that he had something to say to them. He didn't quite know where to begin.

"I guess I shouldn't be so bullheaded," he finally said.

"Oh," Ria said, "let me get this straight. You mean you were wrong?"

"I, um, well, sort of," Loro said. "Anyway, I guess I should listen to you guys once in a while."

Ria grinned. "Well, it's only about time you realized that!"

Trentor snorted in agreement.

"Now that that's settled," Ria went on. "Do you need any help?"

Loro shook his head. "I think I just need to move around a little."

"Good," Ria said, "because we've got plenty of work to do. Mom already knows what happened. She checked you over while you were asleep, and you don't have any broken bones. She's on her way back here right now. We were lucky. Our house is basically okay. You can go home with her while Trentor and I stick around and help everyone who needs us—basically half of Bonabba."

"Half of Dinotopia, I wouldn't doubt," Trentor said. "A typhoon like that doesn't come to just one village—it comes to the whole island. There could be injuries and damage to every village and city, especially here in the west."

"You're so full of cheery news," Ria chided, shaking her head at him. "Trouble is, you're probably right."

It was true, Loro thought. Trentor was like his father in that way. Their precautions were always worth hearing, as was their advice.

"Why don't we start over there, with the twins," Ria said to Trentor. She pointed to a pair of older girls who were picking up the pieces of a barn door.

"There you are!" Katherine said as she approached. "I'm glad you're up!"

"What's left of me," Loro said.

"Come on, let's get you home where you belong," Katherine said. She gave Loro a big hug and a kiss. He leaned on her as they slowly walked home.

The next day, Loro felt much better. His body was still sore and his chest still hurt, but his head felt normal and he could move around.

The pod house hadn't been damaged too badly. One of the windows had been broken, and the spire on the top of the roof was torn off, but that was the worst of it. As Loro sat down to breakfast with Ria and Katherine, he learned that many others, both in Bonabba and elsewhere on the island, had not been so lucky.

"I've just spoken with a young man and woman who traveled here during the night, sent from Chimeerney, to ask for whatever help we could offer," Katherine said. "It seems they were hit harder than we were. Mr. Leroy was up in the forecaster's pod when the storm arrived. He said it was clear to him, before he had to give up his post, that the worst weather passed just south of us."

"Was anyone hurt?" Ria asked.

"No one's sure how many or how badly," Katherine said. "Bonabba is sending a convoy south this afternoon with some supplies. Everyone we can spare is going."

"I'll go!" Loro immediately announced.

"No, you won't," Katherine said. "You're in no shape to go anywhere. We can find plenty for you to do right here."

"But—"

Katherine stopped him with a single look—the one Ria had learned to use now and then. Loro didn't say anything but just let his chin drop.

"Oh, don't start moping so early in the morning," Ria said. "You know she's right. Come on, let's fix some things around here, then go find Trentor."

Loro quietly finished his breakfast, then helped Katherine and Ria clear up some debris and repair a few holes. When they'd finished, he and Ria headed for the sauropod barns.

There they found Trentor helping several larger saurians push aside a long, heavy cart that had been overturned during the storm.

When they stopped to rest, Loro said to him, "You look worse than I feel."

"It's true," added Ria. "You look like you didn't sleep last night."

Trentor nodded slowly. It was clear that Trentor wasn't at his best: His eyes were baggy, and the usual bounce in his step, the bounce that made riding Trentor more than a little difficult, was missing altogether.

"I'm worried about my father," Trentor said. "Traveling across the Rainy Basin is worrisome at any time, but with the storm, who knows what might have happened to them?"

"Your father is extremely large and wearing full armor," Loro said. "And the others in his caravan are almost as experienced as he is. I don't think there's anything to worry about."

"Believe it or not, I have to agree with Loro," said Ria.

"You're right," Trentor told them. "I'm trying not to think about it. But all night I kept imagining him lying on the trail, trapped under a tree just as Loro was. The others couldn't get it off of him. They needed my help, but I wasn't there."

"I have an idea," Loro said. He looked carefully at both of them. "We could form a new caravan and go into the Basin to meet him."

Ria frowned, but Trentor looked thoughtful.

"I also have considered that," Trentor said. "But everyone who isn't injured or caring for the injured is helping put the village back together or going with the big caravan to Chimeerney, including the last of the

Brachiosaurs. There aren't enough people or saurians left."

Suddenly, someone called, "You there!"

They turned toward the voice. A group of villagers had gathered around a nearby pod house. One of the men was waving at them.

"We could use a few more hands and feet!" he said.

"Okay!" Ria called back.

"Later, when we're done here," Loro said in a quiet voice, "maybe we should go to the bridge—"

"Loro!" Ria said with a frown. "Do you have to start with that?"

"—and watch for Fraalor's caravan," Loro went on.

Ria gave him a sidelong glance, then nodded.

"And on the way," Loro continued, "maybe we can try again to talk the adults into letting us go to Chimeerney!"

Ria and Trentor laughed and shook their heads as they joined the repair team. There was no shortage of work to do. The nearby pod house was only the beginning. The three of them spent the afternoon helping bolster two large barns. After dinner, they helped clear a path along the eastern edge of the village. By dusk, they were all exhausted.

But they weren't too tired to do what Loro had been waiting for all day, which was to make their way to the bridge. There they sat and rested and gazed at the place, far on the other side of the ravine, where the cross-Basin trail worked its way into the edge of the jungle. No matter how hard they stared, they couldn't see any movement.

After a long, quiet time, Ria said, "It'll be dark soon."

"When it is, we'll go home," Trentor said. "I just wish I knew whether the caravan was okay."

"There's still only one way to know for sure," Loro said.

Ria scowled at him.

"I haven't decided against going to look for my father," Trentor said. "But there's still the same problem. Without Brachiosaurs for a proper caravan, we're stuck here."

"There must be a way," Loro said.

"There isn't," said Ria.

Suddenly Trentor cried out. "Look!"

"Where?" Loro asked, squinting into the jungle.

"Not there!" Ria said. She pointed into the sky. "*There!*"

Loro looked up and saw it.

"A hot-air balloon!" he said. "I've never seen one quite like that before."

"Neither have I," said Ria.

"Me neither," Trentor said. "I'm sure it's not from Dinotopia."

That, of course, was exactly what Loro wanted to hear.

CHAPTER 5

"It must have been blown here by the typhoon!" Loro said. He squinted into the evening sky and watched the bright red-and-white balloon drift high overhead.

"I wonder where it's coming from," Ria said, watching intently.

"There is someone inside," Trentor announced.

Trentor could see, hear, and smell better than any human, and his eyes were especially good in poor light.

"Just one?" Loro asked.

"I don't know," Trentor said. "I saw movement."

"It's coming down," Ria said. "I think it's dropped a little already."

"And look where it's heading," Trentor said.

They stood silently and watched the balloon descend on the gentle evening breeze. There could be no doubt that it would land deep in the jungles of the Rainy Basin.

"Someone has to go and find that balloon," Loro said. "Can you imagine landing out there in the jungle with giant predators roaming around?"

"That would be a bad experience," Trentor agreed.

"What if they've never even seen a dinosaur before?" Loro added. "Any dinosaur, let alone a Tyrannosaurus or Giganotosaurus! There's no way that balloonist is going to make it alone."

"I hate to admit it again," Ria said, still staring after the vanished balloon, "but I agree with Loro."

Loro held his breath as he turned to look at her. "You do?"

Ria nodded, a very solemn look on her face. "I don't know anyone in Dinotopia who would want to crash in the Basin, let alone someone from the outside world. They won't know the first thing about surviving out there."

"Yes," Trentor said. "And it's likely that whoever's in that balloon will have been without food or water for days. Or they may be injured. Or—"

"I think we get the idea," Ria said, chewing gently at her lower lip, deep in thought. "You know, if there are new visitors in that balloon, everyone will want to meet them."

"Especially you," Loro said.

Ria shrugged, then grinned. "Of course."

Loro shook his head and grinned right back. "You know, I don't think we've all agreed on anything before," he said. They stood there for a moment, listening to the distant calls of night birds and the faint ratcheting sounds of countless grass-dwelling insects.

"This is probably the only village that balloon passed over," Loro said at last.

"Probably," Trentor said.

"And we know that the balloonist, or balloonists, will need help," Loro added.

"Almost certainly," Ria said, her voice strangely low.

Trentor shifted his head to look out over the ravine, toward the jungle. "If they don't get help, they will probably not survive."

The darkness had deepened now, but the sky was already filled with stars, and the crescent moon shed plenty of light. Loro stared at the darkened shapes that outlined the vast jungle on the horizon—a familiar sight to him, but quite alien to someone new.

"That's what I think, too," he said.

"Yes," Ria said, adding a heavy sigh. "And we really can't let that happen."

"Agreed," Trentor said.

"We'll have to tell the rest of the village," Ria continued. "We need to assemble a caravan to send out to find the balloon."

"But there isn't anyone to go right now," Trentor said.

"Hmm," Ria said, pressing her lips together. "I suppose you're right. A proper caravan won't be possible for days. Those balloonists had better hope your father's caravan spots them!"

Trentor shook his head. "As I estimate their landing, they are too far north of the main trail. My father's caravan will not see them."

Loro took a deep breath. "Then we should go!" he said.

Trentor and Ria turned and stared at him, but neither said a word.

"I know what you're thinking," Loro went on. "I know I'm always trying to get you two to go exploring, but this is different. There's someone in trouble. They won't survive without our help, and there's nobody to help them except us!"

"Us," Ria repeated.

"Yes, us," Loro replied. "And we can also look for Trentor's father's caravan. We might meet up with them on the trail. And when we do, they can help us find the balloonist and then get home."

"I hadn't thought of that," Trentor said, clearly interested now. "It might be possible. But we must consider all the problems we might encounter. There are so many!"

"I already did," Loro said. "I've considered every detail a hundred times. I've been ready to set out into the Rainy Basin for a long time now, and, deep down, I think you have, too."

"There's no way we'll ever get permission," Ria said. "We'll probably have to wait for the Chimeerney caravan to return, or at least part of it."

"That is probably the only choice," Trentor

agreed. "Without a trained, experienced guide, you couldn't even consider going."

"Right," Loro said. "But that's not a problem, because we know just where to find one." He looked at Trentor. "You know more about traveling through the Basin than most of the official guides—only your father knows more. And that's not to mention your collection of maps!"

"I do have one of the largest collections of maps in the region," Trentor said, his head swaying from side-to side. "But—"

"The largest collection in all Dinotopia is more like it!" Loro insisted. "And you have the knowledge."

"I do know every one of my father's stories by heart," Trentor said. "But—"

"Every single one!" Loro encouraged him. "Even more."

"But—"

"Trentor, please," Loro said. "Don't be so modest. I would trust you with my life any day! What about you, Ria?"

She squirmed. "Yes and no," she said. "I agree that most of what you're saying is true, but what makes you think for one minute that we—"

"Ria, please, this may be the balloonist's only chance!" Loro said. "Besides, with you along, we're sure to stay out of trouble."

"Well, if anyone is going, I'm going, and that's a fact," Ria pronounced.

"Of course!" Loro said. "In fact, you would have the deciding vote on all the important decisions."

"You'd put me in charge?" Ria asked, clearly intrigued.

"More or less," Loro answered. He waited for the rest—the arguments, the lectures, the trouble. He waited a long time, but nothing happened.

"Well?" Loro finally asked as Ria and Trentor glanced at one another.

"I'm a little worried that you might be right about all of this," Ria said. She looked as serious as Loro had ever seen her. "Which means we might have to do just what you're saying, and that is really scaring me."

"I still think it's too dangerous," Trentor pointed out. No one else spoke. "I can't begin to tell you all the terrible things that might happen to us."

Ria leaned toward him and held his gaze. "So what you're saying," she said, speaking slowly, "is that if Loro and I decide to go into that jungle and rescue the balloonist, and maybe your father as well, you're going to let us go alone?"

Loro glanced at Ria in disbelief.

She gave him a look that told him to keep his mouth shut. Trentor looked as if he'd just stepped on something sharp. He made a strange, groaning sort of noise that resonated from somewhere deep inside his massive skull.

"No, no, no, I didn't say that," he replied. "That's not what I meant."

"It's important, because I'm pretty sure there won't be any stopping Loro from going this time," Ria continued. "And I can't let him go alone. You shouldn't either. My mother gave us strict instructions to keep an eye on him, remember?"

"She did?" Loro asked.

Ria practically snarled at him.

"Oh, I'm sure she did," Loro said. "And she's always right."

"We can't let him go alone, not on such an important and dangerous mission," Ria said.

"No, of course you can't!" Loro agreed.

"You don't have to go, Trentor," Ria went on. "You don't have to help. Even though you're the best chance we have of actually making it there and back, and even though half the reason we're going is to find your father, and even though you're supposed to be our best friend, and even though—"

"No, no," Trentor said, groaning like a wounded Brachiosaur now. He took a long, deep breath. "If you two are going, I will go too, as your guide. And I will do my very best."

Ria nodded. "I know you will," she said.

"You are the very best! You'll be great!" Loro said, almost too excited to think straight.

"Not that I'm saying we're definitely going," Ria added. "There's still one big problem."

Loro froze. "What's that?"

"Our parents. You just wait until we go home and

tell Mom we're running off into the Rainy Basin, even if it is to rescue some balloonist and find Trentor's father."

"I know what my mother will say," Trentor said. "No."

"But can't you just tell her—" Loro began.

"She'll still say no," Trentor replied.

"Our mom will definitely say no," Ria said.

She was right. That's exactly what Katherine would say. So would Danra, Trentor's mother.

"So what now?" Loro asked, feeling a bit ill. "Do we just give up?"

"We could wait for just a day or two, to see if the others come back early from Chimeerney," Trentor suggested.

"By then it could be too late," Loro said. He felt his dreams and hopes slipping away. They'd been so close. "There's just no way, is there," he said.

"Unless…" Ria said.

"Unless?" said Loro.

"Unless we leave a note."

"A note?" Loro and Trentor asked, at the same time.

Ria nodded. "A note telling our mothers where we've gone and why. So they'll at least know where we are. If we're going to do this, it's the only way."

"By the time they read it, we'll be long gone," Loro said. "You're a genius!"

"Of course I am," Ria said smugly. "That's why

you should always listen to me. And let's get one thing straight. I'm doing this because someone's in trouble, and we're the only ones who can help. I'm *not* going because I think charging off on some foolish adventure is a good idea. Got it?"

"Got it," Loro said.

"And *I* am going because of what Ria just said, and because of my father, and because the people in the most trouble will be you two if I don't go," Trentor said.

"I know how worried our parents will be," Loro said, "but when we get back with Trentor's father and the balloonist, I think they'll be very proud."

"I hope so," Ria said quietly.

"Me, too," said Trentor.

Loro looked at his friends. They were actually going to go, for some of the same reasons he was, and the other reasons were as good as any.

Trentor cocked his head to one side. "We have to gather supplies without anyone noticing, and write the notes, and look over my maps, and plan to meet before sunrise, and—let me think—I know there are other things."

"No problem," Loro said. He took Ria's hand in one of his and patted Trentor's snout with the other. "We'll take our time, we'll do everything right, and we'll do everything together, from here on."

"We'd better," Ria said.

"And we'll need a saddle," Trentor said, still thinking, "so I can carry both of you. And we'll need to bring along some baskets, one of them full of smoked fish, in case we run into any meat eaters, which we probably will. If there's room, we should bring a few extra supplies, so that if we find my father and they need help, we will have it."

"Yes, yes, and yes," Ria said. "But we also need to settle on a few rules. I suppose Loro can lead the expedition, more or less, but Trentor should have first say on all trail procedures. We must also be ready and willing to turn back if necessary. And most important of all, I get final say in all critical decisions."

"Loro isn't going to like that," Trentor said.

"No," Loro grumbled, "but I guess I can live with it."

Ria smiled. "Who said you had a choice?"

Fine, Loro thought. It didn't matter. What mattered was that practically every dream he had ever had was about to come true!

CHAPTER 6

As soon as Katherine was asleep, Loro and Ria gathered their clothes and quietly made their way out of the pod house. They crossed the village to the sauropod barns and met Trentor. The three silently gathered the supplies they would need and secured them in packs and baskets. Loro and Ria each wore a backpack. Trentor was fitted with the rest, along with a saddle just big enough for his two friends.

Not that Ria or Loro intended to ride on Trentor's back. They each had two good legs, after all. But if the situation required it, they could ride for a while; in fact, Trentor had made a list of those types of situations.

When they had gathered all they could, they wrote their notes, explaining what they were doing and why, and returned to their homes. Loro and Ria took time for one last, silent good-bye to Katherine. Then without a word—as if saying something might break their spirits—they met Trentor and headed toward the bridge.

No one manned the vertebral drawbridge at night. Built like the neck of a sauropod, the bridge stood straight up until the weight of travelers crossing over brought it slowly down, eventually coming to rest on the other side of the ravine. That way, no unwanted visitors could cross over in the other direction, from the Basin into Bonabba. The only way to cross from that direction was to wait until someone manually levered the bridge into place.

The noise as they crossed, mostly deep creaking and groaning, seemed loud enough to carry all the way to Fireside. The bridge was used often enough during the day, yet Loro never seemed to hear it. He guessed that everyone was so used to the sound that no one noticed it. Still, Loro didn't want to waste any time, just in case someone woke up.

At the other side of the bridge, Trentor and Ria turned back to look.

"Bonabba will be all right, and so will we," Loro said.

"I know," said Ria. Together, the three turned and continued on. Another few yards, and they set foot, for the first time, on the other side of the ravine.

Loro moved to the front and led the group down the trail. In no time they had crossed the near meadows and entered the trees. By the time the sun was rising, they had ventured well into the jungle.

Here the trees were tall and thick. Their tops formed a green canopy high above the travelers' heads.

The shadows blended together, and the sounds of creatures, too many to pick out, could be heard from all directions.

On either side, the jungle plants—bushes, ferns, twisting vines, young trees, and brightly colored flowers—grew in thick harmony, filling in nearly every available space. This was one of the oldest jungles in the world, surely! How many saurians and humans had passed this way? The idea sent a chill up Loro's spine.

He breathed in deeply through his nose. The smell of the place was like every garden in the land rolled into one. The damp earth and plants, the blossoms, the thick mosses that grew on every surface—all mixed together in a rich bouquet. He kept breathing deeply until he realized that doing so was making him dizzy!

"We should stop to observe, look, and listen to our surroundings every half hour or so," Trentor suggested.

"Okay," Ria said. "Let's start now."

They all stopped where they were.

The trail itself was wide enough for two large sauropods to pass one another easily, and it was smooth enough for good footing, as long as you kept an eye out for holes and ruts. Most of the bordering undergrowth stood half again as tall as Loro, but he found that by standing on Trentor's back he could see over it.

"Nothing observed," Trentor said after a few moments. Loro climbed down, and they started off again.

By the time they were nearing the end of their first day, Loro was feeling good, and he could tell that the others were, too. But the setting sun was slowly turning the shadows into vast dark pools, and the calls of birds were giving way to more troubling sounds. When they passed a dense thicket, Loro heard a heavy, skittering sound, like something long and low moving across the ground.

"Just keep moving down the trail, steady and straight," Trentor said. "We are an unusual sight. The curious are many. But most creatures will not trouble us, if we don't trouble them."

"You mean they won't trouble *you*," Ria told Trentor. "Attacking a Styracosaurus would be a mistake for most. But Loro and I would make a much easier meal."

"Not as easy as you think," Trentor said. "Most meat eaters, even the larger ones, eat small game. There is almost no risk in hunting such creatures, and there are many of them about."

"So they're really looking for a meal that's even easier than we would be," Ria said.

Trentor nodded.

"But we're not easy, because humans are unpredictable," Loro added.

"I agree," Trentor said. The corners of his mouth turned up into a grin.

The conversation ended abruptly as a distant but well-defined roar rang out. This sound was rarely heard in Bonabba, or anywhere else in Dinotopia—anywhere else in the world, for that matter. Fresh chills touched the back of Loro's neck. A second roar, almost as far away, drifted on the still evening air.

"The herd is not coming this way," Trentor said.

"But what if it does come this way?" Ria asked.

"That depends," Trentor said.

Loro looked up. "On what?"

"On what I think we should do," said Trentor. "Each situation is different, and so is what you do about it. My father's stories have taught me at least that much."

Loro knew exactly what Trentor was saying. He'd heard and read enough to know that survival depended on many things—swift feet and cunning among them.

"For now we have to find a place to make camp for the night," Trentor said. "That's our top priority."

"Thank goodness," Ria said. "I'm so tired."

Loro nodded. After all, they'd been walking nonstop for an entire day and hadn't gotten any sleep the night before.

Trentor took the lead until he found a campsite that met with his approval. The clearing was not ideal—it was too far from the trail—but Trentor decided that it would have to do.

"Looks good to me," Loro said, trying to ease

Trentor's mind. The clearing was large, at least fifty yards across, and gaps in the surrounding vegetation would make it easy to leave in a hurry if need be. Loro pointed all that out.

"I know," said Trentor. "What worries me is how this clearing was formed. I think it was intended to be a nesting site for some very large saurians. They trampled all this brush and pushed over those trees, but then they must have changed their minds and moved on."

"Sounds good to me," said Loro.

Trentor shook his head. "We don't know why they didn't like it here. We also don't know whether they'll change their minds and come back."

Loro felt his throat tighten, but he tried not to let his concern show. "We'll just hope for the best."

"There's a brilliant plan, if I ever heard one," Ria grumbled.

"Thank you," Loro said with a grin.

Trentor waved his head from side to side, then began pushing grass and leafy tree limbs into a pile. Loro and Ria did the same, making beds for themselves. Then they got blankets out of the packs Trentor was carrying.

"Should we start the fire now?" Loro asked. He'd imagined this over and over in his mind—he and his fellow explorers gathered around a crackling fire, its light reflecting off their faces.

Trentor shook his head. "Fire attracts too much attention."

"Anybody knows that," Ria said, giving Loro a look. "Are you serious?"

"Uh, no, of course not," Loro said. "Just kidding."

As he lay down on his makeshift bed, Loro made a promise to himself to try to think things through a little more carefully on the rest of their journey. There was so much he hadn't considered. He couldn't afford to assume anything, or miss anything, or forget anything.

It was all very hard to remember...

"Good night," Ria said, as she covered herself up with her second blanket. She pulled it over her head to keep the bugs away.

"Good night," Loro said.

"I wonder what our mothers must be thinking," Trentor said.

Immediately, Loro imagined Katherine reading the note on her door. They were all thinking the same thing, Loro knew—how worried their mothers must be—and wishing there had been some other way.

But there wasn't, Loro reminded himself. *We didn't have a choice.* Suddenly, he noticed the noises around him, and the depth of the darkness closing in on all sides. Soon, he knew, it would be so dark he wouldn't be able to see anything. He tried rolling over and thinking about the balloon. For a time, he was fairly certain, he drifted off to sleep…

Then his eyes were open again, peering into the darkness. He heard a rustling in the leaves somewhere beyond the clearing. The sounds faded, then were gone.

Nothing. He lay back down, then turned on his side, then turned again.

He heard Trentor moving about, adjusting his weight on the leafy bed he had made for himself. Ria coughed gently and rolled over.

"Not asleep yet?" she whispered.

Loro turned, but he couldn't see Ria through the gloom.

"Not yet," he said.

"We should just rest, then," Ria said. That was what Katherine always told them on restless nights. Just rest, and eventually they would sleep.

"Yes, rest," Loro replied.

He heard Ria turn again. Then she said, "What are you thinking right now?"

Loro sighed. "You don't want to know."

"No, really," she said. "Tell me."

"Well," Loro said, "I nearly drowned with my parents when their ship went down. In a way, it's like I'm not supposed to be here. But I am here. The dolphins rescued me and gave me a second chance at life."

"And you don't intend to waste it, right?" Ria asked.

"Yeah, but…" He paused, trying to figure out how

to say the rest. "But that's not all. If we do rescue somebody, in that balloon, it's like the dolphins rescuing me. Does that make any sense?"

"Yes, it does," Ria said. "It's one of the reasons I let you talk me into this trip. And one of the reasons I don't think you're completely hopeless."

Loro couldn't see her smile, but he knew it was there.

They heard Trentor move again. "Tomorrow night," he said, "we will take turns keeping watch, so we will be able to sleep more comfortably."

Loro lay back and closed his eyes. He thought about second chances, and how they got passed on from one person to another. Then he drifted until he realized that it was daylight again.

"Time to get up," Trentor said. He was standing over Loro, bumping Loro's shoulder with the side of his great bony snout.

"I'm awake," Loro grumbled, trying to sit up. He felt as though he'd just fallen asleep five minutes ago.

"We have to get going now," Trentor told him, giving him another nudge.

"Okay, okay!" Loro said. "What's the rush?"

"I'm pretty sure," Trentor said, "that we are not alone."

CHAPTER 7

Trentor wasn't sure what was out there, but whatever it was, it was big.

"Allosaurus, maybe, or maybe even a Tyrannosaurus," he said. "Giganotosauruses usually travel in herds, but our new shadow is alone."

"What makes you say that?" Ria asked. She was just about packed and ready. Trentor had gotten her up first.

"I've been listening very carefully. Every once in a while you can hear it walking, a heavy step this way or that. But I hear only one pair of feet."

"That's good enough for me," Loro said, hurriedly finishing his own packing. "Let's go!"

Ria and Loro climbed into the double saddle on Trentor's back. They could travel much faster this way. And now seemed like a good time to travel as fast as possible.

Riding Trentor was anything but fun. At a trot he tended to rock from side to side while jouncing Ria and Loro up and down. The "ups" weren't bad, but the "downs" all ended in a solid, brain-shaking thud. Trentor made good time, though. He kept moving, easily keeping the pace he'd set for himself.

The smells, sounds, and look of the jungle changed as dawn turned to late morning. As the sun climbed higher, the shadows began to shrink, and the movement of countless flying and walking insects could be seen. The birdcalls changed, too, though Loro wasn't sure what species the birds were or what the changes meant. The scent in the air grew richer, as the cool, damp smells of the night air gave way to the warm, steamy aromas of sun-warmed plants.

Despite his worry about whatever might be tracking them, Loro felt a tingle of awe mixed with excitement, just as he had the day before. But today, he decided, the feeling had less to do with the newness of the trail; rather, it was the jungle itself that excited him. It thrived all around him, just as it had for millions of years, and he was a part of it.

"Do you think we've lost our friend?" Ria asked as Trentor paused for a moment along the side of the trail.

"I am trying to find out," Trentor said. "But you both must be very quiet."

Loro and Ria nodded. They got down and listened too, though Loro knew their human ears were not nearly as keen as his.

After a few moments Ria turned to Loro and

shrugged, but the sudden tip of Trentor's head suggested that he was not happy.

"Still there?" Ria asked.

"Yes," Trentor said, "but now I think there may be more than one."

"Do you think," Ria asked, "if we keep moving—"

Trentor silenced her with a grunt that clearly meant *stop* in any language. Loro and Ria held their breath. Then Loro heard it, too. The faint yet titanic thump, thud, thump, thud of a very large dinosaur moving slowly along. Then he heard a second thump, thud, overlapping the first.

He glanced at Ria. She'd heard it too.

"Can't we hide somewhere?" Ria asked.

"Not for long," said Trentor. "The hunters that follow us do so by scent. They can smell us wherever we go. I don't think they're too hungry, though, or they would have had us by now. I think we're still a curiosity."

"Let's hope we stay that way," Ria said.

"We will be all right for now," said Trentor. "They must think we are easy prey. They'll wait until they're hungry, or their curiosity runs out, and then they will either move on—or feast."

"Feast?" Loro said. "But I thought the big predators mostly preyed on the weak, the sick, the old, the stragglers. Not young, healthy, fast-moving—"

"That is true, especially when it comes to the large armored caravans that travel this trail," Trentor said.

He turned his great head in another direction, sniffing the breeze. "And especially if the predators are not starving. But we are sort of in between—and so, I think, are our friends."

"I wish we could disappear," Ria said to herself. Then she leaned close to Trentor's ear. "You must have guessed something like this could happen, so you have a plan, right?"

Trentor nodded. "I do."

"Well, what is it?" Loro urged.

"We will spill our basket of smoked eel and fish meat here," Trentor said. "I am sure those hunters will want it the instant they get a whiff of it."

"Then what?" Loro prodded.

"Then we'll get off the trail and try to get away."

"I like that last part," Ria said.

Loro did too.

"Have you figured this out on the maps yet?" Loro asked. They'd been reexamining Trentor's maps every few hours so far. They'd planned on following the main trail until they reached the area where they would have to veer northward.

"We won't go far from the trail," Trentor said. "And there is nowhere we can go that is not on one of my maps!"

Loro and Ria opened up the basket, then dumped the fifty pounds of fish inside. Its pungent, smoky scent filled the air. It smelled good, Loro thought. They had each hoped to snatch a little for themselves along the way. Now they would have to be content with the dried foods they'd packed and the edible plants that grew in the jungle.

"Okay," Ria said. "Done!"

"Climb back up," Trentor said. "We have to hurry."

The instant the two of them were on his back and in the saddle once more, Trentor left the trail and set off into the jungle. He ran with his nose down, making a trail of his own with his bony skull and ample weight. Loro and Ria were tossed about on Trentor's back and whipped by leafy limbs on both sides. After a few minutes, they all heard a thunderous chorus of roars.

"Giganotosaurus, I'd guess," Trentor said. "But it's still hard to say. There are several similar species of large carnivores that could be after us, and most of them—"

"That's all right," Ria said. "Just keep going. Or is it too late to turn back?"

Loro couldn't tell if she was serious or not, but Trentor was already telling her they couldn't. Not right now, anyway.

"We'd walk right into the jaws of the creatures we are fleeing," he said.

Trentor charged on through the dense underbrush. He kept to a fast trot, just short of a full gallop, which Loro reasoned would have been too dangerous. The ride lasted a long time, long after the contented roars of the feasting carnivores could no longer be heard.

"The wind is with us," Trentor said, when he finally stopped to listen and catch his breath. His endurance was great, but even he had limits. "They cannot follow us easily by scent, and I changed directions many, many times."

"I noticed that," Loro said, trying to get his bearings. For the last mile or two, the land had been getting soggy. Still ponds covered by green algae had begun to appear in the low spots. Where the water grew deeper, the trees were without leaves. Dense brush and bog mosses thick enough to walk on could be seen almost everywhere.

"The water and bogs hide our trail from others," Trentor said.

Loro wasn't particularly fond of swamps and marshes, but if this one offered some protection, he wasn't about to complain.

"So," Ria asked, sounding a little better but still looking worried. "Where are we...exactly?"

Good question, Loro thought.

"We must get out the maps and see," Trentor said. "I'm afraid that, after so much running and turning, I have only a vague idea."

Loro and Ria stared at Trentor in shock. He had only a vague idea?

"Sometimes," Trentor said, "you have to pick one of two poor choices."

"Like getting lost or getting eaten?" Ria asked.

Trentor nodded.

The small, distant squawk of some unknown saurian was the only sound Loro heard for the next few seconds. Trentor looked at them for a moment, then said, "Maps?"

"Yeah, maps!" Loro repeated, trying to get his mind back on track.

It took only a few minutes to thumb through Trentor's splendid collection and find a suitable map. The sun was always a help, of course, rising in the east and setting in the west, so continuing in an easterly direction was easy enough. But they needed to know where the trail was and the best way to get back to it.

"We need a route that will not force us to swim through unsafe waters," Trentor said.

"We're somewhere near here, right?" Ria said, pointing to a spot on the map.

"The east end of the Bogpeat Marsh," Loro said, reading the words handwritten on the paper. It was a very large area, possibly the largest marshland in all Dinotopia, but they were only on its edge now. Which, Loro thought, was far enough.

"We'll go this way," Trentor said, tracing a path across the map with the horn nearest the end of his snout. "Along the edge of this deep pond, then across this area. From these markings, it looks as though the floating bog peat is thick enough to support us, if we spread out."

"You know best," Loro said.

Ria nodded. "We'll go where you say, and the sooner the better. I'd hate to be caught out here in these marshes all night. Talk about facing the unknown. The main trail is bad enough!"

"No argument here," Loro said, attempting a weak grin.

"I'm afraid there's an even better reason," Trentor said. His tone instantly wiped Loro's grin away.

"What's that?" Ria asked.

Trentor's head was up, and he was sniffing the wind. "There is something quite close by that I do not like."

Loro felt his throat ache again as he swallowed.

"What is it?" Ria asked.

"I don't know," Trentor said, "but they are smaller and faster than the large meat eaters we just escaped from."

"Maybe they're not meat eaters," Ria said hopefully. "Maybe they live in the marshes because there are so many plants."

"Perhaps," Trentor said. "But—"

Suddenly, twin screeches sliced through the humid air. Loro spun around to see two forms roughly half Trentor's size scurrying through the brush. Then they leaped out of the shadows, straight at them.

"Run!" Trentor howled.

CHAPTER 8

Trentor led the charge through thick swamp grass. The water was ankle-deep, and the muck below it sucked at their feet.

Loro dodged a thick cluster of hanging vines and suddenly found himself in the lead. Ria ran right behind him. He ducked a clump of branches, then heard Ria yelp and stumble as the branches struck her face. She covered her eyes with one hand while Loro grabbed the other.

"Follow me!" he yelled.

A few steps later they came to a stand of trees and brush too dense to penetrate. Loro went left, and Trentor went right. By the time Loro realized they'd split up, it was too late. The carnivores were still behind them, yelping with excitement.

Loro did his best to keep their original direction in mind as he pushed through the tangled jungle. Ria stayed with him, holding on to his hand.

Suddenly they broke into a clearing and ran headlong into a dark, gooey pool of algae-covered muck.

Loro tried to keep moving, but the muck held him fast. Then his heart nearly stopped—he was sinking!

Loro looked over his shoulder. Ria was just a half-step behind him, and in exactly the same fix. They were both in up to the waist and sinking slowly. The smell of rotted vegetation rose all around them. Loro took a slow, shallow breath, careful not to move any more than he had to.

"Trentor!" he howled. As the air left his lungs, he sank a little more.

"Trentor will come back for us," Ria said in a hoarse whisper.

"We'll be too deep by then," Loro said. "We'll be nothing but two black circles in the green stuff."

"Don't say that!" Ria said. Loro noticed a tear at the corner of one of her eyes. He felt his own eyes stinging with wetness. He hadn't cried in a long while, and he didn't want to start now.

The muck began to press in against his stomach, making it harder to breathe.

Loro took another deep breath. *"Trentor!"*

Suddenly, Loro heard twin snarls. He looked over his shoulder and saw the creatures that had been chasing them—a pair of young Velociraptors! Loro had heard a lot about these saurians. They were energetic, efficient predators that hunted in teams. They used a combination of speed, cunning, and razor-sharp claws on their hind feet to seize and overcome their prey.

Even now, as they stood at the edge of the clearing, the raptors couldn't seem to stand still. They shuffled, hopped, and flexed their foreclaws. Their heads moved constantly as they chattered to each other and watched Loro and Ria.

Then Loro heard a trumpeting noise. He looked forward and saw Trentor's bony face peeking through the reeds across the pond. Behind him, Ria squealed with excitement.

The raptors shrieked as well.

"They've seen him, too!" Ria said.

"Get away!" Loro called to Trentor. "Run!"

"The raptors!" Ria called to him. "Look out!"

Loro looked back over his shoulder. The raptors were watching Trentor and edging along the pool, trying to get to him.

Loro was having more than a little trouble breathing now. He looked down. The muck was halfway up his chest.

"We have to stop moving," he said.

Ria nodded. "What about Trentor?" she asked.

"I have an idea," Loro said. "Keep yelling."

"It'll just drive them crazy," Ria said, gasping between words.

"I know," said Loro. "That's the idea."

"What idea?" she asked.

"You'll see," he told her. "Just do it!"

Ria rolled her eyes, then turned her head toward the raptors again. "Hey!" she shouted.

She trusted him, Loro realized, as he began shouting too. He'd wondered exactly when that had happened. Minutes, days, years ago? Or was it just this second, when she had nothing to lose? But that didn't matter, he decided. What mattered was that they were trusting each other, or trying to trust each other. He just wished it didn't have to be the last thing they ever did…

"Hey!" Ria yelled again.

The raptors were going crazy. They bounced and chattered excitedly, then rushed straight at them. They hit the muck pond at full speed.

Loro and Ria cheered as the raptors sank in up to their slightly rounded bellies. Their deadly hind claws were no longer a threat. But as Ria turned to him again, Loro saw a look he hadn't expected. She looked sad.

"What is it?" Loro asked.

She looked back at the raptors, and Loro understood. The raptors sounded almost like they were crying.

"We had to," Loro said. "We had to save Trentor."

"I hate to see any living thing suffer, for any reason," Ria said. "There's almost always another way."

"Not always," Loro said. He felt himself slip a little deeper into the muck. It was nearly up to his underarms now. Loro glanced across the pond, but Trentor was gone.

"Where'd he go?" Loro asked.

"I don't know," Ria said. Loro almost couldn't

hear her over the raptors' shrieks and howls.

"I hope he gets back okay," Loro said.

"Yeah," Ria said. "Good luck, Trentor." Her voice had begun to shake.

"Be safe," Loro mumbled.

"In the Rainy Basin it is hard to be either lucky or safe," Trentor said.

"Trentor!" Loro and Ria cried.

Trentor stood just behind them at the edge of the muck pond. Beside him stood a creature nearly as big as he was, but quite different otherwise. It had a large, barrel-shaped body and a long, snouty face. Its thick forearms and curving hind legs ended in long, finger-like claws. Its entire body was covered with dark brown fur.

"What is that?" Loro asked, as the great beast began to climb a tree at the edge of the bog.

"She's a giant sloth!" Ria said at once. "I've never seen one—they don't like the more populated parts of Dinotopia—but I've often heard about them. They are peaceful creatures, if you let them be."

"This one is quite nice, really," Trentor said.

They watched the sloth slowly crawl up the nearest tree as deftly as a person might walk across a street. As the sloth got higher the tree began to bend under the animal's great weight. After another moment of climbing, the tree and the sloth were hanging right over Loro and Ria. The creature reached out with one huge front paw, grabbed Loro's arm, and pulled.

Loro heard an enormous sucking sound as the muck lost its grip on him. Suddenly he came free and found himself flying through the air. The ground came up and he crashed into it, right beside Trentor. The thick mosses growing there cushioned his fall. An instant later, Ria landed just beside him. They were both covered in thick, oozing, stinking black muck.

Loro didn't mind a bit.

"Thank you!" he howled, at Trentor, at the sloth, at the entire jungle.

"Thank you, thank you!" Ria added, tears running down her smiling face.

"What did you expect?" Trentor asked, tipping his head in a way that meant he was rather pleased.

The sloth made a rapid series of short moaning sounds as it slowly backed down the tree.

"She said you are both welcome," Trentor translated.

Loro and Ria got to their feet and started hugging each other. Then they hugged Trentor, getting muck all over him. He didn't seem to mind. Their moment of jubilation was cut short by a fresh round of screeching from the pair of raptors. They were now nearly up to their chests in the sticky muck.

"There will be others of their kind about," Trentor said.

"Others?" Loro asked.

"I think so," said Trentor. The sloth made a low moan, which seemed to indicate that she agreed.

"They will come here soon, to help these two if they can. Either way, they will probably come after us."

"That doesn't sound good," Loro said, trying to stay calm. "I guess we should get moving."

Trentor watched the struggling raptors, then nodded heavily.

"The raptors' friends will track and catch us no matter what we do, right?" Ria asked.

"Do you have another idea?" Loro said.

"Yes," Ria said. "Yes, I think I do."

"You're kidding, right?" Loro asked. If she was, he wasn't in the mood. Not only were their lives in danger, but they were also covered with slime.

"No, I'm not," said Ria. "I'll bet they don't want to sink under that muck any more than we did."

"How do you know they'll honor a deal?" Loro asked.

"Dinosaurs do not lie, not even meat eaters," Trentor said.

That was true, as far as Loro knew. But it was one thing to say so and quite another to bet your life on it.

"Let's go talk to them," Ria said. She started toward the raptors.

Trentor nodded and trundled after her. The sloth went with them. Loro had no choice but to follow.

"Ask them," Ria told Trentor. "If they agree, we'll help them get out of the muck. Then they can help us get out of these swamps."

Typical Ria, Loro thought, as Trentor translated the message. Judging by the raptors' excited whoops and squeals, they liked the idea.

Trentor calmed the raptors, then said, "They want their freedom and are only too happy to help us in return. They are quite young. Just children, I think. It seems they were playing with us more than actually hunting us. Their parents feed them regularly and take them hunting for small animals."

"Wonderful!" Ria said, beaming.

"They will help us find the trail again," Trentor went on. "From what they tell me, the way is dangerous. They will go ahead and find the safest route. I think it is the best chance we have."

"Excellent!" Ria said.

Loro rolled his eyes.

"In truth," Trentor said, "I believe the sloth would have helped the raptors anyway, just as she helped us, but the raptors don't know that."

Ria just grinned. Loro grinned a little, too. It was sort of wonderful, come to that. In fact, he wished he'd thought of it.

Trentor spoke again to the sloth. In no time the raptors were standing among the others, dripping dark muck and chattering up a storm. Keeping his eyes on the raptors, Loro slowly slid around behind Trentor. Ria did the same. But as Trentor and the raptors spoke further, Loro realized there was nothing to worry about—at least not yet.

"The raptors want to thank all three of us," Trentor said to Loro and Ria. "Not just for rescuing them, but also for the fun they had chasing us."

"Yeah, sure," Loro said. "Fun."

Ria made a sour face, but then both of them broke into laughter. The raptors started chattering and squealing with excitement all over again.

Everyone thanked the sloth. The creature seemed quite pleased by it all.

"I think she had fun, too," Trentor said.

Then they set about making their way through the jungle again, careful to watch their step and listen to the sounds around them. The raptors led the way, darting ahead and coming back every few minutes.

The raptors took them through a few tangles, then around a large, deep pond, and finally to more solid ground. As they reached a clearing in the trees, the raptors started acting differently. They stood still for the first time, stared at their new friends, then backed away into the trees and disappeared.

The afternoon was turning into evening, and the main trail was nowhere in sight.

"Where did they go?" Ria asked.

"Wait," Loro said. "Did you hear that?" He scanned the jungle on the far side of the open slope ahead of them.

"I smelled something a moment ago," Trentor said, turning in place.

"There," Ria said, pointing off to the right. "Something's moving."

Loro peered into the misty shadows. Here and there, between the leaves, he caught sight of a snout, an eye, and then lots of snouts and eyes! He recognized the shape of the heads.

"More raptors," he said. "A whole band of them."

"They are behind us, too," Trentor said. Four more raptors stood in the shadows a few yards off. They were all around, Loro realized, as still more of them emerged from the jungle.

"It must be a trap," he said. "They tricked us."

"I hope not," Ria said in a strained voice.

"I don't understand," Trentor said. "I was sure we could trust those two."

Suddenly, twin shrieks broke out behind them. They turned to find the two young raptors they'd saved from the muck. Others of their kind came bouncing and skittering closer. Trentor listened intently to their chattering, then turned to Loro and Ria.

"The cross-Basin trail is just beyond those trees," he said. "Our new friends, and their families, have come to wish us well."

CHAPTER 9

The next day proved more productive. The trio managed to travel many miles on the main trail without a single incident. Trentor kept a close eye on his maps, on the trail, and on how close they were to where he thought the balloon had landed.

"Tomorrow," Trentor said, "we should be very close."

It was almost too good to be true. Loro grew more excited with every step.

They spent the night in a very large lean-to on the side of the trail. It had been built as a temporary shelter for passing caravans. Halfway through the night, a light rain made Loro especially glad to have a roof over his head, even if it was only part of a roof. They took turns keeping watch and getting some much-needed rest. Sunrise found them alive and well, and eager to continue.

The new day's march was marked only by the appearance of a herd of strange, furry animals. They

"Is he alive?" Loro asked softly.

"I think he's breathing," Ria said. "Stay here while I check it out." She inched forward, then reached out and grabbed the side of the free-swinging basket.

"Hey!" she whispered, still trying to keep her voice down. "Hey, wake up!"

The boy's eyes fluttered opened and focused on Ria.

Then the boy started to scream.

"Shh!" Loro said, leaning as close as he could.

"Hey, it's okay!" Ria said. "We're friends. We're here to help you."

She looked at Loro. "He's terrified," she said.

Poor kid, Loro thought. He'd undoubtedly never seen a Giganotosaurus before, especially not a whole herd of them, and all trying to have him for lunch. Whoever he was, he'd had a bad few days. He wore simple clothing: a tan tunic, a well-worn pair of loose pants, and leather sandals. His skin was dark and his hair as straight and black as his eyes.

"That's why he's still alive," Ria said, pointing to three water canteens on a hook inside the basket. "He had water. But I don't see any food. I bet he's starved."

"While you're attempting to ask him if he's hungry," Loro said, "try to remember that we'll all be food if we don't get going."

"I don't even know his name," Ria said.

"It...is...Amal," said the boy, in a voice that was even thinner and weaker than he looked.

"Good! Amal!" Ria said. She smiled and held out her hand to the boy. "I'm Ria, and this is Loro. He's right, we've got to get you out of here."

"Was there anyone else with you?" Loro asked, reaching to help Ria hold the basket still.

"No, no one," Amal managed to say, as he dragged himself up off the floor of the basket. Ria and Loro helped him out onto the branch. He was weak and wobbly, but standing.

"The next problem is, it's a long way down," Loro said. "But I've got an idea." Using vines, Loro tied Amal to himself and Ria while Ria gave Amal a few sips of water from the pouch in her backpack. Then the three of them started inching down the tree. Amal did his best to climb, but he mostly just hung between them.

At first Loro wasn't sure they were going to make it all the way to the bottom. But finally, just as the last of Loro's strength was gone, they dropped down and stood on solid ground.

"That was much too difficult," Ria said, trying to smile. "I'm glad it's over."

"Me, too," Loro said, "but the next problem is the herd. I hear some very big footsteps, and I think they're getting closer."

They all listened as the ground shook with distant saurian thunder. Amal started to tremble all over. Loro knew the feeling.

"Head for cover," he said. "We have to find that trail—and Trentor—again."

Ria nodded, and they set off across the clearing. They quickly found the path they'd followed through the jungle and started retracing it. In no time they did find Trentor—or rather, he found them. He came running up behind them at a full gallop. And he had good reason for running: nine good reasons, in fact.

"The Giganotosaurus herd is right behind me!" Trentor yelled.

Ria glanced back. "I think they're gaining," she said.

Amal turned also. When he saw Trentor pounding toward them, he started screaming again.

"It's all right, Amal," Ria said. "He's our friend!"

"Yeah, it's those others we're worried about," said Loro.

"Run! Run!" Trentor bellowed as he got closer. The Giganotosaurus herd thundered after him, crushing everything that was growing in their path. Their footfalls sounded like explosions. Roars from two of the herd's leaders sent chills running down Loro's spine. Loro grabbed one of Amal's hands while Ria kept hold of the other. They bolted down the trail, dragging Amal like a sack of grain.

Trentor caught up to them a moment later. Without a word he pushed past them and took the lead, helping to blaze the trail. It wasn't enough. The herd was still gaining.

"Oh, no!" Ria cried, as Trentor stumbled over a clutch of vines draped across the trail. Ria had no chance to avoid him. With a half step and a bound she let go of Amal and tumbled over Trentor's hindquarters; then she bounced off his head and crashed to the ground in front of him.

Loro rushed to help Ria. Luckily, Trentor got up on his own, as did Amal. Trentor seemed to be favoring one of his front legs.

Loro looked over his shoulder. The Giganotosauruses were right on top of them!

We're not going to make it, he thought.

Suddenly, something twice his size and very fast dashed past.

"Raptors!" Loro shouted, wide-eyed, as at least a dozen or more rushed headlong toward the charging Giganotosauruses. The two young raptors at the back of the pack were the ones from Bogpeat Marsh, Loro realized, as they chattered at him on the way by.

The raptors ran straight into the midst of the Giganotosauruses, darting between their mammoth hind legs and nipping at their haunches. The Giganotosauruses twisted and turned, jaws snapping at the air as they tried to strike back. Loro knew the raptors were fast, but he couldn't believe what he was seeing. No matter how they tried, the best the Giganotosauruses could do was kick over the raptors, mostly by accident. But as soon as that happened, others in the raptor pack would dart in and distract the Giganotosaurus while still others got their dazed companions to their feet.

The raptors moved off into the jungle. The Giganotosaurus herd followed, bellowing furiously. Loro turned to find Ria, Trentor, and Amal all staring after them.

"I think we're supposed to get out of here now," Loro said.

"I don't want to stay here, that's for sure," Ria said.

"No," Trentor agreed, "but we can't stay on the trail either. Eventually the Giganotosauruses will tire of chasing such agile prey, and they'll come after us again."

"What kind of terrible place is this?" Amal asked, taking short, trembling breaths.

"It's not terrible at all," Ria said. "It's called Dinotopia, and it's wonderful! Well, most of it is, most of the time. The cities and villages are—"

"A little dull sometimes," Loro said.

"Well, this is just a little too exciting, don't you think?" Ria asked.

Loro laughed. "Maybe," he said.

"What kinds of creatures are these?" Amal asked, still looking at Trentor uneasily.

"They're dinosaurs!" Loro said, patting Trentor on his haunches. "This is Trentor. He's a nice dinosaur and a good friend. He saved our lives once already on this trip, and he helped us save yours."

"Most saurians are nice," Ria said, "because they've been working on being civilized for millions of years. But some of the dinosaurs on this island, some of the meat eaters, aren't as friendly."

Amal looked at where the trampled vegetation ended, only a few dozen yards from where they stood. He nodded heavily.

"My maps," Trentor said. "We need my maps."

Loro opened the map basket, got out all the maps, and spread them on the ground. Trentor quickly found the one he was looking for.

"There," he said, indicating their position. "A stream flows near here, no more than half a mile to the west. We can wade in the water and follow it a good part of the way back. If the wind stays as it is, it will be difficult for the Giganotosaurus to follow us. They'll lose our scent."

"But before we go very far we're going to have to get some food into Amal," Ria said. She turned to the boy. "How long since you've eaten?"

Amal just looked at her for a moment, as if he couldn't get his thoughts together. Then he said, "Many days. There was no food in the balloon."

"Okay," Loro said, "but first let's get off the trail and put a little distance between us and this place. Then we'll see what we can do about food."

The others agreed, and they set out through the jungle in the direction of the stream. Trentor had a slight limp from his fall, but it wasn't bad.

They hadn't gone far when they came upon a group of gangly, fruit-laden bushes. Bright red berries hung by the thousands in clumps as big as fists, all of them shiny and plump. The patch was filled with the sweet-and-sour scent of berries that had fallen and begun to rot. It smelled delicious.

Amal lunged into the bushes.

"No!" Ria cried, reaching after him. With Loro's help, they dragged him back, away from the bushes.

"Those berries probably wouldn't kill you," Ria explained, "but just a handful would give you a bellyache you'd never forget. Let us pick the menu, okay? We have some food with us, and there are other fruits in the jungle, if you know what to look for."

Amal nodded.

"Wait here," Loro said. He pulled some bread from his backpack. "Eat this. Ria and I will get you something to go with it."

They gathered several pieces of ripe green fruit from the ground beneath a nearby tree. The skin was tough—you had to pull it back with your teeth—but the green-and-white fruit inside was soft and sweet. Loro thought the juices would help replenish some of what Amal's body had lost.

They let him eat as they started toward the stream again.

"We didn't get a chance to thank those raptors," Ria said.

"They probably know we're grateful," Loro said.

"I doubt that we will see those raptors again," Trentor said. "The only way they can lose the Giganotosauruses is to keep going until they are out of the herd's territory. After a time, the hunters will give up the chase. Then, they'll probably try to find us again."

"I hope they take their time," Ria said.

"Yes," Amal said, looking from Loro to Ria to Trentor. "Hope."

"I wish I could carry all three of you," Trentor said.

"I know," Ria said. "I know."

A distant howl, low and loud, echoed among the trees. Another one answered from somewhere closer by. Loro felt a familiar chill touch his spine.

Hope, he decided, was not much to go on.

CHAPTER 11

Trentor's father, Fraalor, and his armored caravan had not seen home in many weeks. They not only had braved the perils of the Rainy Basin, but also had been forced to weather a violent typhoon—a storm the like of which Fraalor had never seen. Its floods and rushing water had made a part of the trail impassable. Fallen trees had blocked their path. Fortunately, the last leg of the journey had been easier.

Even so, as the peaks of Bonabba's highest roofs came into view beyond the edge of the jungle, everyone let out a joyous cry.

"I wonder if the village was spared the worst of the storm," Fraalor said to Tamta, the lead Brachiosaur. Tamta had been with Fraalor on every cross-Basin journey he'd ever made.

"The village has withstood many a storm, some nearly as terrible as this last one," Tamta said. His long neck swayed gently back and forth as he walked, making the armor plates he wore clank and clatter in a constant, gentle rhythm.

"I'm sure you're right," said Fraalor, "but I worry all the same, especially about my family."

"As do I, old friend," Tamta said. Tamta had never taken a mate, but he came from a very large family. Even his great grandparents were still alive. This was not unusual among saurians.

"Very soon now, we will know," Fraalor said, as they approached the dividing ravine. Already, the bridge was beginning to drop down to allow the convoy to cross. A good sign, Fraalor thought. Also, he could smell food cooking on a fire, something that meant home as much as anything else. He hurried the pace slightly, unwilling to slow down despite his sore feet.

They crossed the bridge and headed straight for the sauropod barns. There Fraalor found his wife, Danra, rushing to meet him. They butted muzzles, then leaned into each other. They said hardly a word.

When Fraalor looked up, he saw Katherine, the mother of one of his son's best friends. She was waiting just beside him. He decided that the look on her face was not joy. As he turned to his wife, he saw the same look in her eyes.

"It's Trentor, and Loro and Ria, too," Katherine said. "They saw a hot-air balloon crash into the jungle and went to rescue the pilot."

Fraalor felt his insides grow heavy. "Go on," he said. "Tell me everything you know."

Fraalor listened intently as Katherine and Danra

explained. Like everyone else, Fraalor understood why the children had gone, though no one thought it best, no matter what the circumstances. He waited silently until he had heard all Katherine and Danra had to tell.

"It is not a good sign that we didn't see them on the trail," Fraalor finally said, wishing he had something more encouraging to say. The concerned looks on the women's faces deepened.

"Then...you don't think they're...alive?" Katherine asked.

"I didn't say that," said Fraalor. "Sometimes we leave the main trail. Trentor knows all the reasons, and they may have discovered a few of their own. We could easily have missed each other."

"They thought they had to go," Katherine said. "They thought there wasn't anyone else to rescue the balloonist."

"I know, I know," Fraalor told her. He turned and looked about. By now, the Brachiosaurs would be back in their barns and removing their armor. They were weary and in need of rest. If he asked, Fraalor knew that his old friend Tamta would put the chafing armor back on and accompany him to the ends of Dinotopia. That was exactly why he couldn't ask.

"I'm going after them," Fraalor told Katherine and Danra. "I will have to go alone."

"No," his wife insisted. "Two mistakes will not fix one! What good will it be if you are lost as well?"

"I am going. There is no time and no choice," Fraalor said. "Help me pack my carrying baskets with what fish can be found, and food and water. Please."

No more persuasion was needed. While Fraalor ate greens and drank juices, the two women filled a basket with chunks of shark meat and smoked eel. They fixed it on Trentor's back as he prepared to go.

When all was completed, Fraalor nudged his wife one more time. "I will come back," he said. Then he told Katherine, "I will find them. I promise."

"We know," Danra said.

Fraalor turned and walked over the bridge once more, back onto the cross-Basin trail, back into the jungle.

CHAPTER 12

The walking went slowly, especially when the four friends reached the stream and tried to wade in it. The rocky bottom was slippery, slowing them even more. Thankfully, it had been some time since they'd heard any sound of the Giganotosauruses.

Amal was feeling a bit better now, with a belly full of ripe fruit and dry bread. He walked on his own, and needed help only when his balance failed him. Loro stayed between Ria and Amal, where he could help either one of them if need be.

While they walked, they talked. Amal wanted to know how they had found him.

"We saw your balloon sailing over our village, and Trentor figured out the rest," Ria said. "We knew you were landing in a trouble spot. That's why we came to rescue you. We knew you'd need help."

"Yes, help!" Amal agreed.

"But we want to hear all about you, Amal," Ria said. "Tell us where you come from, and how you ended up in that hot-air balloon."

"Well," Amal said, "I was born in a country called India, but I have not been there for many years."

"Did your family move?" Loro asked.

"I did not know my parents," Amal said. "I was an orphan."

"So was I," said Loro.

"Where did you live?" Ria prodded.

"When I was four, I came to belong to a man called Hansman," said Amal. "I don't remember much before that. He is a healer, or, I mean, he tells people he is. But I am not sure he can truly heal anyone or anything."

"Then what makes him a healer?" Trentor asked.

"He claims to know the ways of nature and the uses of healing herbs and plants. He sold his medicine in the villages wherever we went. Once, he nearly sold me!"

"What?" Ria said, eyes wide. "He tried to sell you? I don't understand."

"I have heard of this in stories some of the elders tell," Trentor said. "It is a human thing, owning another of your kind. I believe it is against the laws of many lands, though not all. It is hard to imagine."

"Very hard!" Ria said, shaking her head. "I mean, what kind of man—"

"Not a good man," Amal said. "He made me work very hard for him, day and night. I was a servant, nothing more."

Loro tried to imagine what his life might have

been like if he'd lost his parents somewhere else, other than here in Dinotopia. He'd long thought of a day when he might travel to faraway lands and find adventure, but suddenly he wasn't sure he liked the idea.

"He called himself the Healer, but I have heard him called other things, bad things," Amal continued. "Once, he was attacked by men who called him a swindler."

"Is he rich?" Loro asked. "I've heard that some people in your world are very wealthy."

Amal thought for a moment. "He often had money," he explained, "but he often lost it. He liked to play games with cards. Many times, he lost more money than he had."

"What were you supposed to do for this man?" Trentor asked.

"Whatever he said, whenever he said."

Ria tipped her head to one side. "And what did you get in return?"

"Food, most days," said Amal. "And these clothes."

Loro glanced at Ria and Trentor and saw the troubled looks on their faces.

"That's a lousy deal," Loro said.

Trentor and Ria agreed.

"Why didn't you seek help from others?" Trentor asked.

"Others?" Amal asked.

"Yes," said Trentor. "Others in your community or the communities you visited."

"We lived in places for only a few days," Amal said. "Poor places. I knew no one, and few would have helped me if I'd run away from Mr. Hansman."

"Things must be very different in those places," Trentor said, shaking his big head. "And much more frightening."

Ria frowned. "I just wouldn't do what Hansman asked until he treated me better," she said.

Amal shook his head. "Then, he would give me nothing, except perhaps a beating."

Ria gasped. "What an evil man!" she said.

"It does sound that way," Trentor agreed.

"Where is he now?" Loro asked.

"Yes, why wasn't he in the balloon?" Ria asked. "Did the Giganotosaurus herd get him?"

"I was alone," Amal replied.

"It must have been a terrifying flight," Trentor said.

"I think flying in one of those would be fun," said Loro.

"You would," Ria said. "Amal, tell us what happened."

"I was traveling with Mr. Hansman through a strange land," Amal continued. "Jungles much like this one grew up to the edges of the cities, but most of the people lived in villages like those in India. The villagers' skin was more yellow than brown, and their faces were strange but gentle. We came to a small port city at the edge of a southern ocean. Many people from a land called England were there. Some of them owned the balloon. Mr. Hansman won the balloon from them in a card game that lasted three days."

"Three days!" Loro said. "They must take card games very seriously."

"They do," said Amal. "They hardly slept or ate."

"So then what happened?" Ria pressed. "How did you end up in the balloon?"

"Mr. Hansman told me to sleep in the balloon so no one would steal it during the night. It was tied to the ground at the edge of town. I did as I was told. But just after I reached the balloon, the wind started to blow and the sky grew dark. It happened so fast!

"Mr. Hansman came running into the field and grabbed hold of the balloon's ropes, but he did not think that would be enough. He saw some men walking along the edge of the field and told me to stay in the balloon. Then he ran after the men. Suddenly I felt the balloon going up. It was pulling the stakes out of the ground! I called to Mr. Hansman, but he was too far away and did not hear.

"A moment later he returned with the men, but they were too late. A strong gust of wind pulled the balloon completely loose, and it started to rise. Mr. Hansman shouted at me and the balloon and even the storm, but the balloon kept going up. I wanted to jump out, but already the balloon was too high."

"I would have jumped out anyway," Ria said.

"Definitely!" Loro agreed.

"He was afraid to stay and afraid to go," Trentor said, giving Amal a gentle look.

Amal said, "Yes. Mr. Hansman was so upset that he was losing the balloon. He kept yelling and jumping up and down."

"Didn't he notice that he was losing you, too?" Ria asked.

"I think so," Amal said.

"Please go on," Trentor urged.

Amal took a breath. "One of the men tried to tell me how to fly the balloon, but I couldn't hear him. I hung on, and the balloon went very high! Then it flew out over the ocean, and the basket started to fill with rain. I was afraid I would drown. When I stood up, the wind tried to push me out of the basket. It was as if the storm was trying to throw me out so it could eat me alive!"

"Sounds awful," Ria sympathized.

"We had a little trouble with that storm ourselves," said Loro.

"But you stayed in the basket, and the balloon stayed in the air?" Trentor asked.

"When the storm calmed, the balloon was very high up," Amal said. "It was so high that the clouds were underneath, not above. But then the balloon began to fall. There is a fire in the top of the basket, but I could not find anything to light it with. I thought I would fall into the ocean, but then this land appeared beneath me. The wind carried me again until I landed in the tree with the monsters around it."

"And we know the rest," Loro said.

Everyone was quiet for a moment, thinking over Amal's story.

"Nothing like that could ever happen in Dinotopia," Ria finally said. "Here, people and dinosaurs care for each other. Everyone works hard to make it a good place."

Ria glanced at Loro and raised her eyebrows. "Of course, some work harder than others."

Trentor snorted. "I'm sure Amal thinks that Loro helped."

Ria smiled. "I guess you're right."

"I'm lucky to be here," Loro said to Amal, "and now you are, too. There are plenty of people who will welcome you to our village of Bonabba. All we have to do is get back."

"For now, we need to rest," Trentor suggested. They had come to a group of fallen trees that would be very nice seats.

"Your family," Amal said, sitting beside Loro. "Do they worry about you while you are in such a dangerous place?"

"Um…" Loro said, feeling a twinge of guilt. "Yes, a little, I'm sure."

"He's sure that if we don't get killed out here, my mom will kill us when we get back," Ria said.

"She will?" Amal asked, shocked.

"Something like that," Ria said. "We left a note for them, but..."

Loro glanced up. Ria and Trentor looked miserable. Loro felt the same way.

"Maybe we should get going again," Trentor said.

"Yes," Ria said, despite having just sat down. "Maybe we should."

Everyone got up and trudged through the stream once more. By the time the four emerged from the water, it was nearly dark. They spent the night not far from the main trail. Though the rest was welcome, no one got very much sleep.

The morning was warm and bright, and Amal seemed to be feeling better. After only two hours, the group emerged onto the cross-Basin trail.

"We made it!" Ria cheered. The wide-open trail took the jungle back yards, instead of inches, for the first time in days. Loro and Amal were smiling and nodding. Only Trentor didn't seem caught up in the moment.

"What's wrong?" Loro asked him.

"We are still a long way from home," Trentor cautioned. "There are many problems we may yet have to face. There is the threat of predators, for one, and—"

"We know, we know," Loro said.

"Yes, we do, and we thank you for thinking about it," Ria said. "But we've survived a lot already. We went deep into the Basin, we found the balloon, we saved Amal, and, with a little help we got away from a herd of hungry Giganotosauruses!"

"It is true," Trentor said. "We have done very well. In fact, if our luck doesn't change—"

A sudden rustle from the trees down the trail stopped him short. He turned this way, then that, sniffing the air and listening intently. No one moved or made a sound.

"There," Trentor finally said, turning to face directly down the trail. "Something is coming."

CHAPTER 13

Loro stared down the trail. He could see something, a saurian of some kind, moving slowly towards them. It didn't look like the larger meat eaters they'd encountered, but it was still too large to be most of the smaller kinds. No, it looked more like a...

"You know," Loro said, "if I didn't know better, I'd say that was a Styracosaurus. But what would a lone Styracosaurus be doing out here in the middle of the—"

"Hooo!" The shout came echoing up the trail.

Trentor stiffened in surprise, then started running down the trail. "It's my father!" he howled.

"Who?" Amal asked, peering down the trail. "What?"

"Fraalor!" Ria said, already starting after Trentor. "Trentor's father has found us!"

Loro and Amal jogged after the others. Trentor and Fraalor hooted and bellowed at each other in a duet of delight. Fraalor was just as glad to see Ria and Loro. Then he paused to consider the stranger. Trentor introduced Amal. With help from Loro and Ria, he started to explain how they had rescued Amal from the downed balloon.

"That's why we came," Trentor said, talking as quickly as he could. "Loro and Ria decided they had to try to rescue the balloonist, and of course they needed a guide. So, after weighing everything that might happen if they tried it alone, which I could never let them do because I'd never forgive myself if something happened to them, and after—"

"Yes, yes! Enough!" Fraalor said. "I am aware. But are you aware that your mothers are near collapse with worrying about you? And with good reason. You are all lucky to be alive. I don't think you realize how many terrible fates await you in these jungles."

"Oh, but I do, Father!" Trentor said. "And I told them, several times. I'm sure you know of even more dangers, but they start with the weather, and the meat eaters, and getting lost, or sinking in black muck, as we learned too well, or—"

"Or wandering into infested waters, or being attacked by insect hordes," said Fraalor.

"Or taking ill, or getting separated," Trentor said.

Loro looked at Ria and rolled his eyes.

"However," Fraalor said, "that does not excuse any of you. I admit that you've done quite well. Rescuing this boy is a most commendable deed. Trentor, I am proud to say that you will make an excellent guide one day. But that day has not yet come. I can assure each of you that this will not go unpunished, and if anything like this happens again, no matter the why or the wherefore, you will all be—"

His speech was cut short by an unwelcome but by now all too familiar sound—a chorus of Giganotosaurus roars. Everyone turned to look down the trail. The herd broke cover and pounded out onto the main trail just a hundred yards or so to the west. They were blocking the only way home.

"They've found us again!" Loro gasped.

"Hmm," said Fraalor. "They've been very active this season."

"Yes, very active!" Trentor agreed.

"Don't worry, Amal," Ria said. "We'll figure out what to do. We've got the two best trail guides in all of Dinotopia with us."

She turned to Trentor and Fraalor. "Okay, so what are we going to do?" she asked.

Trentor looked at his father. "The fish meat?" he suggested.

Fraalor cocked his head. "We can only do that once. I was hoping it wouldn't be so soon."

The ground started shaking as the Giganotosauruses moved closer.

"I have an idea," Loro said.

Everyone looked at him.

"Run?" he said.

"Yes, run!" Fraalor said. "We'll try to circle upwind, then find a place to hide."

They ran straight into the jungle, darting between tree trunks and moving through dense under-growth—places where the huge Giganotosauruses couldn't easily go. Behind them they heard timber snapping as the Giganotosauruses forced their way through.

"This herd is very large," Fraalor said between breaths. "And very hungry. They will be hard to lose no matter what we do."

Ria moaned.

"We're going to have to use the fish meat," Fraalor said. "We'll go back toward the main trail and dump the basket out in the open, where all of the Giganoto-sauruses can get at it."

Everyone agreed, so Fraalor changed directions and led the way back toward a point on the trail where they could emerge safely—for a moment at least—and dump the basket of fish.

The thick jungle held the herd back a little as the group hurried along. After a moment, they stumbled into a clearing. Loro could see the cross-Basin trail just beyond.

"This should do," Fraalor said.

Loro and Ria quickly opened the basket on Fraalor's back.

Amal stared at the fish. He was shaking all over.

"What's wrong?" Ria asked.

"The amount is so small," Amal said. "Those crea-tures are so large, and there are so many of them."

Fraalor grunted. "You're right, but at the moment this is our best chance for escape."

The pounding of the herd was getting closer. Loro cleared his throat. "Time to scatter this meat and make a run for it," he said.

Fraalor bent slightly while Loro and Amal reached for the basket.

"Wait!" Ria said. She was staring intently at some bushes at the edge of the clearing.

"What?" Loro asked.

"Just leave the fish in there for now. I've got an idea, but I'm going to need everyone's help!"

"This has to work," Ria said, keeping her voice low. She, Trentor, and Amal watched the clearing from behind some bushes. Fraalor and Loro sat at the edge of the clearing, waiting.

Suddenly, the Giganotosauruses crashed through the jungle and into the clearing. The great beasts towered over Fraalor and Loro, eyeing the prize that was nearly theirs.

Loro quickly cut the ropes holding the fish basket and dumped its contents. Large chunks of shark meat and smoked eel tumbled to the ground.

"Go!" Loro yelled.

Fraalor galloped away and never once looked back. Behind him the entire herd of Giganotosauruses leaped onto the meat. They bent down and gulped the chunks in a frenzy, swallowing great mouthfuls at a time To Ria's surprise, they even ate the basket!

"Let's go!" Loro yelled as he and Fraalor charged past. "We won't get another chance!"

Trentor quickly followed, with Amal and Ria on his back.

"They'll pick up our scent as soon as that fish is gone," Fraalor called back. "Then they'll be after us again."

"*If* your plan doesn't work," Loro said to Ria.

"It will," Ria said. "It has to!"

Suddenly, Fraalor stopped and cocked his head to one side.

Trentor did the same. "I think I hear moaning and groaning back there."

"Yes," said Fraalor. He waited only a minute or so, and then led everyone back the way they had come. They crept to the edge of the clearing and peered through the bushes.

The Giganotosauruses were howling, swaying from side to side, and stumbling into one another. They sat on their huge hindquarters and tried in vain to rub their bellies with their stubby forelegs. All of them looked flushed. The moans and groans were getting louder.

"It worked!" Ria said.

"Yeah, but there's only one problem," Loro said. He held out his arms. "We may never get these berry stains off our skin."

Ria looked down at her hands and arms. She was

stained from her fingertips to her shoulders from stuffing red berries as far as she could into the big chunks of smoked eel. Loro looked the same. Amal was red only to the elbows, having stuffed berries into shallow cuts in the shark meat.

"Next time, we'll think of a plan requiring feet," Ria promised with a grin.

"We'd better get moving again," Loro said. "In a few hours those beasts are going to start feeling better, and I bet they won't be happy."

"No," Fraalor agreed, "they won't. Let's go."

"We're going home now," Ria told Amal. The five of them started back toward the main trail once more. "I think you're going to like it there."

"Yes," said Amal. "I think I am."

CHAPTER 14

The group made good time getting home. By late the next day they'd managed to reach the jungle's western edge without incident—if you didn't count Fraalor's continued lectures and Trentor's unfortunate propensity to help. At least Fraalor had stopped talking about the events of the past few days and was instead talking mostly about the future.

"This won't happen again, no matter what. Agreed?" he pressed.

"Oh, it won't," they all answered.

Amal asked lots of questions about everyone and everything in Dinotopia. Fraalor spoke at length of the history of the island's saurian culture, which dated back over one hundred million years. Trentor talked about his place among his kind and how he planned to fill it.

"It must be wonderful to belong to such a huge family," Amal said. As far as Loro could tell, he was talking about the whole Styracosaurus species.

"It is," Trentor said. "It is."

Loro talked about how lucky he was to have found a new family here. Ria talked about why there had never been any question regarding taking Loro in—or any regrets, other than the fact that lately they practically had to nail his shoes to the floor to keep him from rushing off into the jungle or beyond.

"But his desire to go rushing off was very fortunate for me," Amal said, bringing a smile to Loro's face.

Soon, they'd left the jungle behind and started across the open grassland. A very large and familiar drawbridge stood in the distance, and beyond that a welcome sight: Bonabba. Home.

As they crossed the bridge and entered the village, Loro felt all the energy drain out of him. It was as if he were a boat and the sail had just been lowered. Still, he felt good. Very good.

"I get to introduce Amal to everyone!" Ria insisted.

"Of course," Loro said.

The others nodded.

A crowd of saurians and humans started running the moment they spotted the band of returning travelers. Some ran toward them in welcome; others ran away, to spread the word. By the time they'd reached the middle of the village, it seemed that everyone had come out to see them. Danra and Katherine quickly pressed to the head of the crowd.

Cheers filled the air. Tears of joy ran down Katherine's cheeks and Danra's wide bony muzzle. There were more than enough hugs to go around.

"They found this one in the balloon!" Fraalor announced, pushing Amal forward. "Ria has already nearly made a citizen of Dinotopia out of our new friend."

"His name is Amal!" Ria said. "And I have so much to tell you about him!"

"She does," Loro agreed. "And I have a lot to tell everyone, too."

Fraalor had pushed up next to Danra and was leaning against her now, as he had done only a few days before. Then he turned and raised his voice to address everyone present.

"Of all the stories that are told," he said, "theirs is, and always will be, one of the best. It's a story all should hear. But it will take time to tell. Later, we will have a gathering, and they will tell the story from beginning to end."

"For the first time," Katherine said, holding both Ria's and Loro's hands. "But surely not the last."

"Amal's story will be told as well!" Ria said.

Cheers rose up again from the gathered crowd. Katherine let go and started to applaud as tears came once more. Loro looked around him and realized that for the first time in his life he was doing what he had always hoped to do. He'd had a great adventure, one that brought some good—a kind of good he could do, a contribution all his own.

Everyone was smiling and talking among themselves. The sun had nearly set, casting long, soft shadows over the village. A cool breeze had begun to blow in from the ocean. Loro looked back across the bridge toward the Rainy Basin and to the sky above. There were no clouds passing overhead this night, but he could see many stars. He listened to the sounds of the jungle and dreamed of things to come.

ABOUT THE AUTHOR

MARK GARLAND has been a lifelong fan of science fiction. In addition to two Star Trek novels, he's written three original fantasy novels and dozens of short stories.

Mark lives in upstate New York with his wife, their three children, and a cat.

SOME FAVORITE
DINOTOPIAN SAYINGS

"To have strong scales." =
To be tough, to have thick skin.

"To roll out of the nest." =
To leave the island.

"To crack through the shell." =
To pass into adolescence.

"A rolled-up scroll." =
Someone whose behavior is puzzling or unpredictable.

"Something is boiling in the pot." =
Something is brewing.

"To look at someone from horn to tail." =
To look someone up and down.

"To be in the horsetails." =
To be lost or overwhelmed.

"To be in someone's scroll." =
To be in good with someone.

"Sing and it will go away." =
Take your mind off your troubles.

"Jolly-head." =
Amusing fellow.

"Head-scratcher." =
Worry, problem, difficulty.

"Breathe deep, seek peace." =
Farewell, peace be with you, take it easy.

Look for these other Dinotopia titles...

WINDCHASER
by Scott Ciencin

During a mutiny on a prison ship, two very different boys are tossed overboard—and stranded together on the island of Dinotopia. Raymond is the kindhearted son of the ship's surgeon. He immediately takes to this strange new world of dinosaurs and befriends a wounded Sky-bax named Windchaser. Hugh, on the other hand, is a sly London pickpocket who swears he'll never fit into this paradise.

While Raymond helps Windchaser improve his shaky flying, Hugh forms a sinister plan. Soon all three are forced into a dangerous adventure that will test both their courage and their friendship.

RIVER QUEST
by John Vornholt

Magnolia and Paddlefoot are the youngest pairing of human and dinosaur ever to be made Habitat Partners. Their first mission is to discover what has made the Polongo River dry up, and then—an even more difficult task—they must restore it to its usual greatness. Otherwise, Waterfall City, which is powered by energy from the river, is doomed.

Along the way Magnolia and Paddlefoot meet Birch, a farmer's son, and his Triceratops buddy, Rogo, who insist on joining the quest. Together, the unlikely four must battle the elements, and sometimes each other, as they undertake a quest that seems nearly impossible.

HATCHLING
by Midori Snyder

Janet is thrilled when she is made an apprentice at the Hatchery, the place where dinosaur eggs are cared for. But the first time she has to watch over the eggs at night, she falls asleep. When she wakes up, one of the precious dinosaur eggs has a crack in it—a crack that could prove fatal to the baby dinosaur within.

Afraid of what people will think, Janet runs away, hoping to find a place where no one knows of her mistake. Instead, she finds Kranog, a wounded hadrosaur. Kranog is trying to return to the abandoned city of her birth to lay her egg, but she can't do it without Janet's help. Now Janet will have to face her fears about both the journey ahead and herself.

LOST CITY
by Scott Ciencin

In search of adventure, thirteen-year-old Andrew convinces his friends, Lian and Ned, to explore the forbidden Lost City of Dinotopia. But the last thing they expect to discover is a group of meat-eating Troodons!

For centuries, this lost tribe of dinosaurs has lived secretly in the crumbling city. Now Andrew and his friends are trapped. They must talk the tribe into joining the rest of Dinotopia. Otherwise, the Troodons may try to protect their secrets by making Andrew, Ned, and Lian citizens of the Lost City...for good!

SABERTOOTH MOUNTAIN
by John Vornholt

For years, sabertooth tigers have lived in the Forbidden Mountains, apart from humans and dinosaurs alike. Now an avalanche has blocked their way to their source of food, and the sabertooths are divided over what to do. The only hope for a peaceful solution lies with Red-stripe, a sabertooth leader, and Cai, a thirteen-year-old boy. This unlikely pair embarks on a treacherous journey out of the mountains. But they are only a few steps ahead of a human-hating sabertooth and his hungry followers—in a race that could change Dinotopia forever.

THUNDER FALLS
by Scott Ciencin

Steelgaze, a wise old dinosaur, has grown frustrated with his two young charges, Joseph and Fleetfeet. They turn everything into a contest! So Steelgaze sends them out together on a quest for a hidden prize. But someone has stolen the prize, and the two must track the thief across the rugged terrain of Dinotopia. Unfortunately, their constant competition makes progress nearly impossible. It's not until they help a shipwrecked girl named Teegan that they see the value of cooperating—and just in time, because now they must face the dangerous rapids of Waterfall City's Thunder Falls!

FIRESTORM
by Gene DeWeese

All of Dinotopia is in an uproar. Something is killing off *Arctium longevus,* the special plant that grants Dinotopians long life—sometimes over two hundred years! As desperate citizens set fires to keep the blight under control, Olivia and Albert, along with their dinosaur partners Hightop and Thunderfoot, race to find a solution. But Olivia is secretly determined to claim all the glory for herself. In her hurried search for answers, what important questions is she forgetting to ask?

THE MAZE
by Peter David

Long ago, a raptor named Odon left Dinotopia's society to live in caverns beneath the island. In order to keep out intruders, he created a dangerous maze. Despite their fears, Jason, Gwen, and a witty young saurian named Booj are determined to reach Odon. Gwen's father is suffering from a deadly disease, and Odon, once Dinotopia's wisest healer, is their last hope for a cure. Will the three friends make it through Odon's maze? And even if they do, how will they ever convince this mysterious hermit to help them?

REVISIT THE WORLD OF

in these titles,
available wherever books are sold...

OR

You can send in this coupon (with check or money order)
and have the books mailed directly to you!

❑ *Windchaser* (0-679-86981-6) $3.99
by Scott Ciencin

❑ *River Quest* (0-679-86982-4) $3.99
by John Vornholt

❑ *Hatchling* (0-679-86984-0)..................... $3.99
by Midori Snyder

❑ *Lost City* (0-679-86983-2) $3.99
by Scott Ciencin

❑ *Sabertooth Mountain* (0-679-88095-X) $3.99
by John Vornholt

❑ *Thunder Falls* (0-679-88256-1) $3.99
by Scott Ciencin

❑ *Firestorm* (0-679-88619-2) $3.99
by Gene DeWeese

❑ *The Maze* (0-679-88264-2)...................... $3.99
by Peter David

❑ *Rescue Party* (0-679-89107-2).................... $3.99
by Mark A. Garland

Subtotal....................................... $ _____
Shipping and handling........................... $ 3.00
Sales tax (where applicable)...................... $ _____
Total amount enclosed .... $ _____

Name _____
Address _____
City_____State_____Zip _____

Make your check or money order (no cash or C.O.D.s)
payable to Random House, Inc., and mail to:
Order Department, 400 Hahn Road, Westminster, MD 21157.

Prices and numbers subject to change without notice. Valid in U.S. only.
All orders subject to availability. Please allow 4 to 6 weeks for delivery.

Need your books even faster? Call toll-free 1-800-793-2665
to order by phone and use your major credit card.
Please mention interest code 8702B to expedite your order.

A WORD FROM DINOTOPIA® CREATOR JAMES GURNEY

Dinotopia began as a series of large oil paintings of lost cities. One showed a city built in the heart of a waterfall. Another depicted a parade of people and dinosaurs in a Roman-style street. It occurred to me that all these cities could exist on one island. So I sketched a map, came up with a name, and began to develop the story of a father and son shipwrecked on the shores of that island. *Dinotopia,* which I wrote and illustrated, was published in 1992.

The surprise for me was how many readers embraced the vision of a land where humans lived peacefully alongside intelligent dinosaurs. Many of those readers spontaneously wrote music, performed dances, and even made tree house models out of gingerbread.

A sandbox is much more fun if you share it with others. With that in mind, I invited a few highly respected authors to join me in exploring Dinotopia. The mandate for them was to embellish the known parts of the world before heading off on their own to discover new characters and new places. Working closely with them has been a great inspiration to me. I hope you, too, will enjoy the journey.

James Gurney